JAKE'S GOLD

Phyllis Hegland

PublishAmerica
Baltimore

ISBN: 1-4137-0386-0
PUBLISHED BY
PUBLISHAMERICA, LLLP.
www.publishamerica.com
Baltimore

Printed in the United States of America

This book is dedicated to my husband Arnold, my son Kenneth Spurgeon, my stepson Steve and his family Mary and Erik Hegland, Gladys Chase, and to the many friends who believed in me and Jake Stone.

Many Thanks.

CHAPTER ONE

HE STOOD THERE, his deformed and hunched back sagging. Wind, sweat and sand were caught in his beard, turning it from black to the gray of dead earth. He squinted his eyes against the glare of the hot sun and glanced at his soiled and ragged clothes. The boots on his feet afforded him little protection against the hot desert sands and rocks. Beside him stood two tired, ragged mules. Dust and sweat had turned them into the same dead color as the man they followed. They seemed a ghostly effigy to that great and mighty desert.

Beyond him, as far as the eye could see, was a barren waste without a blade of grass or a drop of water. The way had been littered with the remains of those that attempted this route before him and he was undecided as to the prospect of his own survival if he proceeded in this direction.

There was, he knew, a better road with grass and water but it would take him miles out of his way and perhaps months from the gold fields of California.

He pushed on. The past years of toil and hardship gave him

an edge over those who left their soft lives in the stores and lush farms of the east to feverishly follow the cry of "GOLD." Their lack of knowledge of the harsh ways of the west was evident for miles. Jake Stone had passed a great many animals dead or dying, their eyes sunken in their sockets, pitifully asking for help. Even in death with flesh torn by vultures and rotting, they seemed to cry for help. The cruel desert had already bleached the bones of emigrants and the remains of wagons, household goods and harnesses were scattered along the dusty trail.

Stumbling along, himself perhaps the victim of a wrong decision, he encountered two mules that staggered up to him moaning and gasping for breath. The sight of their intense agony distressed Jake but he had not food or water to spare. Taking his rifle from one of his packs he mercifully ended their suffering.

Jake led his mules up a small hillock of sand and there stopped to stare into the distance. Ahead of him was perhaps ten or fifteen miles of flat land composed of baked earth and salt incrustations. As he traveled across them, he could see where pits had been sunk in the moist places, but only bitter briny water had afforded the efforts of those who dug them.

It was a foolish decision he had made to make this journey alone. How much better it would have been if he could have attached himself to one of the wagon trains that had gone before. Surely some of them had made it to the gold fields of California. He was grateful for the two hardy mules that had been his constant companions for the last three years. They had spent many months out of each year coursing over every kind of terrain. Even now as Jake staggered along, salt caked to his lips and eyelashes, he was glad his animals were in as good a condition as he.

It was not more than a day and a half later he came across a spring welling up out of the desert floor. The water was cool at his source, warming as it pooled under the sizzling rays of the sun. Moisture spread out over several acres nurturing thick grasses in its wake.

Several wagons had made camp around the little spring allowing their families and teams a much needed rest. There was enough grass to produce good grazing for the weary and hungry animals.

Jake tipped his hat saying, "Howdy, would you mind if my animals and I join your group for a spell? We could use a little rest and the mules would be ever so grateful for the water and some of that grass." He slapped his hat against his leg causing a cloud of dust to fly. His arm wiped sweat and mud from his forehead. Smiling, he extended his hand. "My name is Jake Stone."

A tall man reached over and shook his hand. "Howdy, name's Blake and yer welcome to sit a spell. Give them mules a go at that grass and they'll be ready to go again in no time."

"Thank you, we'll take you up on it. Where are you all bound?"

"Most of us will be heading to Sacramento. A few will be headed to Bodie. I hear it's a rough place, full of thieves and outlaws. I imagine we'll hear the story of Bodie tonight. See that man over there in the stripped shirt? He and a couple of men pulled into camp last night. Claims he knows all about Bodie and is going there to write about it for his paper. He has some interesting stories."

That night Jake lazed around the campfire listening to the story of Bodie.

Mr. Wyatt, the newspaperman, settled down near the fire and rolled a cigarette, lighting it with a twig from the fire, leaned back against a saddle and began his tale.

"It all started when gold was discovered by a man named Willian Bodey and his partner, Black Taylor. The two men crossed the Sonora Pass in the spring of '59 to prospect the eastern side of the Sierra Nevada range.

"They were rewarded with rich looking diggings and decided to build a small cabin and spend the winter. Bodey perished in a blizzard and was not found until the following spring by his partner, Black Taylor. Taylor was later massacred by renegade Piute Indians at the mining camp of Benton.

"The Bodey claim attracted other prospectors and on July 10, 1860, mining laws were recorded in the Mono District for the 'Bodey Mining, State of California.' It was through a spelling error made in the official records in 1862 that the name 'Bodie' originated. And though the man for whom it was named never lived to share in its wealth, 'Bodie' was the name that was to remain with the town from that time on.

"During the years 1860 to 1877, Bodie was in the height of its building boom. The Bunker Hill Mine is the largest single operation at that time. It has been rumored that four brothers had purchased it for the tidy sum of $67,000. It was the fabulous production of this mine that has attracted the wild migration to Bodie. Now, if luck will just run in our favor, we should be there by the first of May."

Jake leaned back on his blanket with his head on his arm and reflected back to the times and reasons that brought him on this long chase after the elusive yellow metal.

He was born in Philadelphia, the thirteenth child of a rather well-to-do baker. At the early age of six months he came down with a fever that ravaged his body. Doctors at that time could find no reason for the fever nor any cure. After many months they noticed a slight curvature was developing. By the time his seventh year had passed and many recurring bouts with high fevers, it was evident Jake was going to be a hopeless cripple. His back was horribly deformed, leaving him crooked and hunched. To compensate for his body weakness, the young boy developed the strength in his arms and legs to a Herculean point. He also developed his mind far beyond his fellow students. This made him unpopular with children his own age, leaving him virtually friendless.

Somewhere around his tenth year he was painfully aware of his parents' shame of him and his deformity, when he heard they were trying to find means to rid themselves of him.

From then on he was met with rejection wherever he went. The desire to prove himself a whole and capable human being became an obsession but wherever he went he was met by ridicule and humiliation. Finally, in desperation, he packed a few belongings and headed west. By then the obstacles in his life taught him to live by wit and skill. He was fast with a gun and possessed great physical stamina and endurance in spite of his crooked back.

The gold strikes of California gave him the fever to strike it rich, return to Philadelphia, buy a business and run his highfalutin, no good brothers out of town.

CHAPTER TWO

THE WAGON TRAIN remained at the oasis for two more days before packing up and moving on. Ahead of them lay some of the worst desert and yet another peril, Indians. Jake was glad for the comfort of the small wagon train for the remainder of the journey. They were to come across much evidence of earlier attacks, which caused the men to keep their eyes open and their guns loaded.

The wagons moved on through the burning desert for several days, reaching the first incline to Montgomery Pass where some of the wagons turned west and headed for the high Sierra Mountains on their way to Sacramento. By this time Jake had made fast friends with the half brothers, Bill Alder and John Smith, who did not seem to mind his deformed back. They invited him to join them on their mining adventure. They figured three sets of hands would work better than two.

Jake accepted willingly. The eldest of the two had been there before and was acquainted with the territory. It gave Jake a feeling of ease and a small finger of belief in his goal.

Another day's travel brought them to Mono Lake, a large body of water in an almost dry desert. The south and west shores were flanked by fir and pines, the north shore supported a busy sawmill. Desert spread out beyond to the east. The waters of Mono Lake, though non-poisonous, were non-drinkable, filled with alkaline and other disagreeable minerals.

The wagon train camped that night at the little settlement of Mono before proceeding around the lake and up into the hills of the high desert to Bodie. It was a rugged climb up those dry craggy hills. The crooked and rut filled wagon tracks that made up the road were worn deep with traffic by proceeding wagons and made it a rough one to follow.

Small dry rock mines were scattered around the hills, with no more than one or two men to each claim. The air was filled with the sound of pick, shovel and the grinding sound of cradle rockers. The hills echoed the waves of sound and filled the valleys with a vibration that brought out the sweat of excitement on the faces of would-be prospectors aboard the wagon train. One by one, as the gold fever became too strong to ignore, wagons pulled off to find their own spot to mine.

Jake's heart was beating hard and his face was wet with the sweat of anticipation. Streaks of salty mud were running into his eyes, his breathing was just short of hyperventilating. Good God, would Bill never stop so they could get on with what they came for. Finally Jake could stand no more. "Bill, when are we going to stop? We're about the only wagon left."

"Not until we reach town, Jake, there is much to see and much to pick up and I don't want us to make any sorry moves. Take a look around you, man, like over there, look at the condition of that man."

Jake looked in the direction Bill was pointing. There, leaning against the rocks was a miner, his clothes were so badly worn they were threadbare. Patches were sewn upon patches and were falling off. He was emaciated and haggard, but still the old fool was feebly moving the rocker arm of a cradle rocker no longer filled with dirt. His eyes were vacant and his cheeks gaunt. The only life left in him was the spark of gold fever still burning in his blood.

"Do you want to end up like that? Even before you get started?"

"Well, no, but…"

"But nothing, the first thing we're going to do is set up some kind of lodging to face the winter with. Now, let's head on to Bodie."

The first thing they saw when they crested the hill was the Bunker Hill Mine and Mill. A little farther on down and to their left were many buildings in the process of construction. The sawmill was perhaps the busiest place other than the mine, in Bodie.

Jake was surprised, he expected to see more people than there were. This was good, it gave them a better chance at the choice spots. Bill assured him that there would be plenty of people as soon as the Sonora Pass was free of snow.

"Right now the only thing I'm interested in is finding a place for us to build ourselves a hut," Bill kept insisting.

The small wagon bumped and rumbled on down the hill into Bodie where they purchased cement, some staples, a few pieces of lumber, boots and some semi-fresh vegetables from one of the freight wagons. Bill turned the wagon around and headed west out of town.

"Hey," Jake yelled, "here's a good spot, Bill. Bill? Hey, Bill, where the hell are we going?"

"Look over there," John said, "doesn't that look like a good spot? Why don't you look where I'm pointing? Gawd damn it, Bill, where in the hell are we going? We're almost an hour out of town now as it is. Why don't you answer us?"

Bill stopped the wagon, heaved a sigh and answered, "Jesus, you fellers are sure full of questions and no brains. Haven' I been tellin' ya that I know where I'm goin' and what we're goin' to do first after we get there? Now, it's just down the road apiece, so hang in there. Haaa! Move along there mules, haaa!"

John and Jake slumped on the wagon seat grudgingly for perhaps another fifteen minutes, then...

"There you are, fellas, right up there, on the high side of that hill. See how there is a hollow spot where it's been blasted out by some other miner? The back of that pit goes straight and down, making a strong back for the hut. No one would be able to sneak up on us from behind. Now that's where we're goin' to build our hut."

It was impossible to get the wagon right up to the spot so, leaving the wagon by the side of the hill, they unfastened the mules and hauled the supplies up by mule back.

Once there, John and Jake became uncontrollable. They wanted to hunt for gold and no amount of talk on Bill's part was going to change their minds. It finally resolved into a fistfight ending with sore jaws and wounded feelings before Bill could make his point.

"Now, I told you before, it's of the utmost importance that we build the best shelter we can. The weather up here in the high desert is fierce. Believe me, I know what I'm talking about." The three men set about gathering small rocks, mixing cement and building a foundation of sorts.

"Now, I figure we should chop off some more of that hill to make the back wall of that hut. Then cement these rocks together for the walls. We'll use the lumber we bought to make the roof. We're gonna have to buy some tarpaper to seal up the cracks in the roof. I forgot about that." Bill was waving his arms and walking around the foundation as he explained the plan. We can use some of the tarpaper to cover the back wall to keep out the water and cold."

It was dark by the time they smoothed out the back wall and all were tired and hungry. Firewood was scarce and they barely found enough to build a good cooking fire.

"Looks like we're gonna have to haul some firewood if we intend to eat and keep warm," Jake said, putting his hands at the small of his back and stretching the kinks out.

"We can gather wood along the trail tomorrow on our way to town," John mumbled as he poured water in the coffee pot. He turned in circles and finally asked, "Where's the food? Did we leave it in the wagon?"

"I don't see it anywhere," Jake replied, "I'll walk down and see if I can find it." It was troublesome traveling, dark plus uneven ground and his deformed body caused him to slip and fall to the road. Swearing softly he picked himself up and climbed into the wagon. Swearing again he cursed himself for forgetting a light. He fumbled around until he found a bag under the seat. He knew it had food as the aroma of bacon tickled his nose when he opened it. Slinging the bag over his shoulder, he climbed down and headed up the hill. The way up was easier, thank God, than the way down.

"I found the bag under the seat. I know there's food in it, I can smell the bacon." Jake put the bag on the ground by the fire. John opened the bag and pulled out the bacon slab and a can of beans with it. "Looks like it's beans and bacon for tonight. Tomorrow I'll go check out the wagon, or maybe one of these boxes will have flour in it and I can make biscuits for breakfast."

While John and Jake busied their selves with the laying of the rock walls, Bill hitched up the mules and went into Bodie for tarpaper. The construction of the little hut took all of seven days. Bill made a huge fireplace that became the whole west wall. On the other side of the fireplace was another room. It was made of clay and stone, large enough to house the mules in the extreme winter months. Those sturdy little animals were the best investment a prospector could have in that country and well worth taking care of.

The roof was made of lumber, sod and wet clay covered with tarpaper. Through it wandered a chimney of sorts. There was one door, east opening, one window, south opening. They built bunk frames under the window and a double-decker against the wall close to the door. Crude as it was, it was one of the best and most comfortable huts in those hills.

Upon completion they began their search for gold. After several disappointing days digging and crushing sample quartz, they came upon a sizable vein of gold. With great excitement they staked out their claim. It was then they made their one fatal mistake. They sent Jake to Bodie to file the claim rights.

Bodie's reputation had drawn many outlaws, thieves and con men. Front men or leads, hung around the assayer's office gleaning information from the poor exuberant miner who, overjoyed at his find, loudly proclaimed the area, amount and grade of ore. Then mysteriously, overnight, the miner and his family would disappear along with the gold he had mined.

Now, here was Jake, excited but not talking too much as he filled out assay forms. He walked out of the assay office reading the papers that were given him, paying no attention to the sidewalk lizards. But the sight of the little hunchback made the thieving lizards see him as an easy mark. They did not have to gain information about him. He was noticeable anywhere.

The three men worked their claim through the hot summer months with ample amounts of rich ore taken and divided equally. They weighed the ore and figured there was approximately $30,000 worth of gold, or perhaps more.

It was difficult to adequately gage the exact amount and they were not about to take it to the assay office for confirmation.

"Okay, now what do we do?" asked Jake. "You say we dare not take it to Bodie, where else do we take it?"

"Well, I say we take it to Carson City. It's a long way to go but safer."

"If it's so safe, why doesn't everybody take their gold to

Carson City?" John asked.

"Most miners are in a hurry to turn their ore into cash and do not want to be away from their claim for any length of time. Now with us, I would say, let's leave Jake at home to guard the mine. He has worked hard and probably could use a little rest time for his back."

"That's a good idea." Jake sighed as he sat down on his bunk and leaned forward placing his elbows on his knees.

John brought out canvas bags and they packed the ore in them.

"I suppose we should wait until after supper to go," Bill remarked, walking the floor and wringing his hands. "We'll eat, pack the mules and then be off."

"You act nervous, Bill, do you expect trouble?"

"Hell, Jake, I always expect trouble where gold is concerned. This is bad country and you never know who's behind the next bush. It's going to be a worrisome trip." Bill finally sat down at the table blowing air from puffed cheeks. "Guess you could say I'm scared to death."

John fixed a supper of boiled potatoes with onions and some very tired looking carrots. He fried up the rest of the bacon and made biscuits. What was left over from the meal they packed in oil treated bags for the trip.

Heavy twilight invaded the valley by the time Bill and John headed for Carson City. Jake stood outside and watched them leave until he could no longer follow their movement. Turning he entered the hut, cleaned up the supper dishes and retired to his bunk for the night.

The days went by and Jake busied himself chipping away at the rock and quartz from the diminishing vein of gold bearing ore. *Well*, thought Jake, *don't tell me that's all there is to that. Can't be, there was too much and we haven't taken out enough for it to play out already.*

Pushing his hat back on his head and wiping the sweat from

his brow, he sat down on a pile of rocks to think.

Turning his head he stared at the shallow hole he dug, then followed the trail of the vein with his eyes up to where he and the boys had first found color. It was an erratic course going first right, then left, then on down the hill to where he was standing. I wonder what I should do now, go left or right. Squinting his eyes, he narrowed his vision on a spot ten feet back from the diggings and noticed color at that point. He remembered when they were digging there, the color was so spotty that they continued on down the hill coming on to richer gold bearing quartz. Jake felt a little quiver of excitement. Gathering up his pick, shovel and the small cast-iron pot he used to crush up the ore, he headed back uphill.

He threw down his tools, picked up the shovel and began digging deeper into the earth. He stood up staring in amazement, the color had run out. He dug to the left, nothing. Okay then, I'll go right, ah-ha! A small spattering of color showed in the quartz. Taking his pick he worked slowly and deliberately in a circular motion. This looks like it could be productive. Placing a sample in the iron pot and using the broken off crowbar, rounded off at the bottom, and proceeded to crush up the quartz. Not bad, he speculated, not as good as the first strike but fair.

Jake was so engrossed in what he was doing that he did not notice the lateness of the day. He hated to give up and was quite a distance from the hut so decided to spend the night at the diggings. They had done that many times before. He walked back down the hill to get the lantern they often used when working late. His stomach was beginning to protest but Jake paid it no attention.

Lighting the lantern, he placed it beside the spot he was working and chipped away at the quartz. Bent over and deep in concentration, he failed to hear footsteps approaching. By the time he was aware of them he had not time to pull his gun

17

before he saw a spit of fire, felt the burning of hot lead in his gut and darkness overtook him.

CHAPTER THREE

CONSCIOUSNESS CAME WITH the feeling of the sun burning hotly on his legs. He slowly opened his eyes, gazing through blurry pain into the clear blue eyes of Pete Dunning. Pete and his family had built a shanty across the dry wash from the stone hut. Though they had little contact with each other, John had shown an interest in Pete's oldest daughter, Jessie.

Jake winced as Pete lifted his head and offered him a cup of water. "Doggone there, Jake, ya sure gave us a turn fer awhile. Thought ya were a gonner fer sure. Me and the boys heard gunshots the other night from over yonder and found ya layin' there jest a bleed'n ta death. We throw'd ya inta the wagon and brung ya home. Dug one slug outta yer belly and another outta yer shoulder. Lucky fer ya they didn't hit nothin' important."

Jake shut his eyes, conscious of the pain in his shoulder and stomach he drifted off to sleep.

A few days later when Jake could sit up and talk, he questioned Pete.

"Have you heard anything of Bill and John?"

"Well, reckon I have, son, this will come as a great shock to ya but I found the dead mules and the remains of the boys about two miles out yonder. I ain't been able to quiet Jessie down since I found them. She was right fond of John. It appears they did away with all your gold, too."

Jake leaned back on the cot and closed his eyes. *Oh God, what happened?* Jake thought. *We never had even a sign of trouble. How did they know?* There had to be someone watching all the time in order to know every move they made.

As Jake lay healing, his mind was devising a way to get his own small cache out of the area without himself being killed.

He looked over at Pete who was working hard at some contraption. What the hell was he doing? It seemed to be a kettle of some sort set into an iron box. Inside the box was a glowing white-hot fire. He mixed something and placed it in the kettle, stirring vigorously. Pete pulled a paddle up dripping with gold and reached for a round mold lined with sheep fat, placing it beneath a spout located on the lower part of the kettle. He opened it and a stream of liquid gold poured into it.

Pete glanced up from his work and drawled, "Wal, now, ain't ya ever seen a smelt before? Learned this little secret from an old prospector friend of mine."

As Jake watched, he wondered why these people used so much sheep fat. They used it for almost everything. Even the dressing Pete used for Jake's wounds was sheep fat boiled down and braced with medicinal herbs and chemicals. Pete changed it often because the fat picked up a rancid smell.

A week or so later when he could walk, Jake headed for home, creeping cautiously along the base of the hill where he could keep an eye on the hut. If any murdering claim jumpers had taken possession, he would see them. He waited and watched. Empty! Climbing slowly and laboriously up the hill, nervously holding his breath, he entered the hut. Apparently no one had been anywhere near since he left. Could they possibly be unaware of the stone hut? Jake flopped down on his bunk and dead tired with the effort of the climb home, slept the afternoon away.

With the morning there came a change in the weather. A cold wind was blowing sand against the window and under the door. Jake lay there remembering Bill Alder's words, "Believe me, boys, I know what I'm talking about. The winters here are terrible and we need strong shelter and a heavy supply of wood." At that moment he was deeply grateful for Bill's wisdom and fighting persistence to "do that first." In his present condition he could not have built a grass lean-to or carry a matchstick to start a fire, let alone build the comfortable quarters he now enjoyed.

He stayed close to home for many days. Watching his ample stock of supplies dwindling, he realized that before winter really set in he was going to have to replenish them and lay in more firewood. Most of his tools were gone and most of his food. His clothing was made for summer and not fit for the coming winter. The only problem was, he did not dare show himself in Bodie at this time.

He knew the mine had been completely taken over and was being worked. His gun was gone and the one he did have belonged to Pete. He lived in fear of being discovered. There was still a small amount of gold hidden in the hut if he could just find some way of getting out of here to buy supplies. The thought of moving from the area was out of the question.

As he lay there dreaming, he heard a resounding clap of thunder and the heavens opened up with torrents of rain. Water collected at the top of the hill and rolled down with the gathering speed of a freight train into the hut and swamping the room. Jake leapt to his feet and with the help of an ax dug trenches around the room and out the foundation. As he did so the sparkle of gold hit his eye. Grabbing the only pan available he began panning the runoff. Working frantically for the rest of

October he managed to collect a fair amount of gold dust.

By the beginning of November the worst of the thunderstorms seemed to be over and the seriousness of his needs became obvious. He thought of Pete and wondered if he could buy one of his sheep to help ward off starvation. Putting on his coat, he went off down the hill, his mind reflecting on Pete Dunning, family man from Texas. Pete said he was here in Bodie after being chased out of Texas for running sheep on cattle grazing land. It had been a short bloody fight and Pete's oldest boy, Ralph, had been killed during the battle. Most of his herd had been slaughtered and he had been given twelve hours to get out of the state.

From the scattered remains of his once bounteous flock, he was able to round up about fifteen sheep. He and his wife set about packing, and, along with their nine children, left Texas. Now that Ralph was gone, most of the remaining children were girls. Jake had to chuckle remembering Pete's remark, "Dang, how could a man be plagued with so many women!" The family had struggled through the desert making friends with an old miner who told them stories of the fabulous gold strikes that were being made in Bodie. The family followed the old miner and it was from him that Pete learned the art of smelting. They had been here in Bodie for two years now and managed to find and smelt quite a fortune.

Jake understood there had already been two raids on Pete's place but the most they ever found was what he was smelting down that day. They never could find the main store of gold.

When Jake arrived at Pete's, he found him busy at his smelting pot.

"By Gawd, Jake, ya look mighty fit," he drawled, going back to his work. "I'm kinda surprised ta find ya still in these parts. Hadn't heard from ya, thought I did see smoke several times, comin' from the hut."

Jake hunched himself over the fire to warm his hands.

"Yeah, I guess you could say I'm still here but I won't be around for long if I don't get some replacements on my food supply. I was wondering if you would sell me one of your sheep for meat?"

"Why shore, you know I'd be glad to. They're starting to get their winter fat. When you get to boilin' him down, I'll show you how to melt down the fat and get all that good oily grease, the greatest dressing for wounds you can use. Any medicine you put into that grease can be packed into any wound to heal, hell, it'll even draw pus outta boils."

"The hell ya say," replied Jake. "You mean all that damn greasy stuff you had all over me was sheep grease?"

"Yep." Pete wiped his hands as he turned saying, "Say, how about some supper? You stay and eat and we'll do some plannin' later."

Later that evening, Jake led his mule up the hill to his hut. There was enough flour, sugar, salt, coffee and dried beans to last until he came back from Carson City. He had promised to replace the staples he borrowed from the family plus bring some much needed goods back with him. Tomorrow they would kill the sheep and dress it down.

As he pulled the stubborn little mule up the hill he was conscious of a growing pain in his teeth. "Damn, another tooth gone bad," swore Jake.

CHAPTER FOUR

THE WIND OUTSIDE howled dismally around the little hut. Fighting the wind and the door he finally unpacked the mule, dumping the supplies in the middle of the room. He then secured the mule in the side room, slammed the door and fell gratefully onto his bunk. Sleep played elusive games with the pain in his tooth, increasing until it felt like every tooth in his head was throbbing. Suddenly he sat bolt upright in his bed. "That's it," he hollered. "By God, I'll do it! I'll go down to Pete's and tell him my plan." The rest of the night he tossed miserably between sleep and pain.

Early the following morning he dressed and took off down the hill for the Dunning place.

"Hey, Pete. Come out here. Let me tell you my plan."

Pete, pulling on his pants as he came, grumbled, "Gawd damn, man, couldn't it wait until after breakfast?"

"No," said Jake, "come over here."

As they walked over to the smelting pot, Jake said, "Pete, I want to ask a favor of you. Do you think you could teach me to melt down my gold and build some forms and make me a plate and set of false teeth outta this stuff?"

"False teeth! What the hell are ya gonna do with a whole mouthful of gold false teeth?"

"I'm gonna get out of these hills with my gold, that's what I'm gonna do."

"False teeth?"

"Yeah, false teeth."

"Jesus, man, ya won't be able to open yer mouth or shut the damn thing once it's open."

"That's okay, just tell me you can do it."

"Wal, by Gawd, we'll try," Pete said, smiling and rubbing his chin.

"Now, what I need to do first is to borrow your tooth puller and get rid of all the stumps and teeth in my head."

Pete disappeared into the shack to later emerge with the "tooth puller."

Everyone disappeared while Pete, amidst much swearing and hollering, pulled Jake's remaining teeth.

Bleeding profusely, Jake took off for his place where he packed his mouth with rags soaked with Pete's magic grease and lay down to dream of his brilliant idea.

Pete and Jake worked together making forms for the gold teeth. First thing was to find some kind of material they could use that would be soft yet firm enough to measure the inside of Jake's mouth. Clay would never work and the sheep fat would just melt. It was Pete's wife, Alice, who presented the answer. Dough. Plain old bread dough. Made without yeast and quite stiff, it could be inserted into the mouth where Jake could bite down to make the impression. It could then be molded to form pockets in which the gold would be poured to make the teeth. The gold would then be poured into the mold after it had dried. Once the gold had set the mold would be broken to expose the teeth. It was a brilliant idea.

Well, brilliant or not, it was easier said than done. They used almost as much dough to get the impressions they needed as Alice did making the week's bread. The unwieldy dough stuck to everything and Jake's saliva made the top and bottom stick together. They finally came up with the proper consistency and by making the top and bottom separately, ended up with a fair representation of false teeth.

They resembled master craftsmen setting hunched over the pliable dough with some of Pete's fine surgical instruments. They poured the melted gold into the doughy plates and put them aside. They used more dough to form a mold for the teeth. Almost all of the gold Jake had smelted was used to perform the task. They fashioned teeth using Pete's delicate instruments and carefully placed them into rounded out holes in the gold plates.

Jake wondered where Pete acquired the fine instruments and also where he came upon the knowledge of healing. Pete looked up as he felt Jake's eyes watching him.

"What's on yer mind, Jake, yer watchin' me like ya never seen me before."

"Was wonderin' where you got these fine instruments and learned so much about healing."

Pete looked up into Jake's dark eyes, then smiled. "I guess I could tell ya. Long ago my uncle was a doctor in Texas. There came a real epidemic of the pox and him bein' the only doctor for many miles around, he worked day and night savin' folks until he worked himself into a heart attack from which he never recovered. My ma, his sister, kept all his instruments and medical books in hopes I would some day follow in his footsteps. But Pa was poor and there never was enough money to see to my schoolin'. Only an abundance of work on a ranch that was already overworked. By the time I was thirteen Ma had died and her hopes and dreams died with her. Pa died a few weeks later in a cave-in in the well he was diggin' in hopes of findin' more water. I was tired of working land that was already worn out, so I packed my belongin's and headed out into the world. Now, that's how I got those fine instruments and if we don't quit jawin', we're never goin' ta finish these molds."

The smelting down of Jake's gold and the forming of the teeth took about four days. There was still gold dust left and he figured if this trick worked and he came back alive, he would plan another trip.

The teeth were atrocious! They were large, heavy, gagging and distasteful. It was evident he was going to have to get used to them before he left. Also he was going to have to keep his mouth shut if accosted by anyone, for the sparkle of the teeth by firelight or sunlight would blind even the sun. Pete and Jake looked at each other and burst out laughing. It took some filing and smoothing to keep the teeth from gagging him. They were going to have to be more comfortable for him to wear them at all times.

The day finally came when he figured he was ready. Shaking hands with Pete, hugging Alice and the four girls, he led the mule out on the trail heading for Carson City.

CHAPTER FIVE

JAKE FELT A thrill of excitement as he locked the door. He did not fear for the hut. One thing, in this country they might jump your claim or murder you for your gold, but one man never broke into another man's house. It was a strange code that existed here. He knew, when he returned, the hut would still be there just as it was now, but he felt safer locking the door.

What a strange grotesque sight he was. The air had turned cold and he was bundled tightly, making his body even more deformed looking. He had a rag tied around his head and tucked under his hat, partly to keep his mouth closed and his jaws from aching as well as appearing to have a toothache.

After giving the Dunnings farewell, Jake struck off west of town to keep as much distance between himself and the townspeople as he could. He passed a few claims where miners would grab their guns and watch him with suspicion. Upon seeing the dismal looking figure with his jaw tied up, they laughed and resumed their digging. Jake was not bothered much that day and saw no suspicious looking men. As night fell he started looking for a safe ravine or outcropping to camp in. He walked up a small ravine which appeared to come to a dead end.

As he approached the end he heard a noise. It sounded like the intake of air from someone who was startled. He stopped short and fear ran over his body in waves, leaving his hair standing up and goose bumps covered his flesh. He waited and listened. To his left were several large boulders and he felt instinctively that someone was hiding amongst them. If they were thieves, why didn't they jump him? In the diminishing light he could see something red. Taking his rifle and cautiously creeping up behind the boulder, shoved his rifle into the red cloth.

"Come outta there with your hands up," he called. With that, there came a sharp cry and Jake dropped his rifle to his side. "My God, a woman!" He stood there in complete shock.

She was hardly more than a girl, dressed in a red satin dance hall gown that had been ripped from her shoulders. She clutched the remains of the bodice to her bosom with shaking hands. Her golden hair had come loose on one side and rippled to her waist. She stood shivering, waiting for Jake to do something and as he made a move forward, slipped to her knees in a faint, exposing herself to the waist.

Jake turned to the mule and untied his blankets. Going over to the girl he slipped an arm around her. He was conscious of her soft white breasts and covered them gently. He stood looking down at her and wondering what the hell he was going to do now.

Walking behind the boulders he found a flat area where he could build a small fire which he had not wanted to do for fear of drawing attention to himself. He hunched around looking for some kind of dry wood with which to build the fire.

It was almost dark by the time he returned and he found the

girl sitting up with the blanket tightly drawn around her shoulders. She watched intently as Jake built the fire. He must have painted a frightening picture with his hunched back and bandaged jaw. He fixed a place for her to sleep and motioned for her to lie down. She eyed him with suspicion and moved over to the bed.

Jake took his rifle and with his back to a boulder sat down to watch and rest for the night. The girl stared at him across the fire. "You're a quiet one, ain't cha?" Jake nodded and settling his hat down over his eyes, pretended to go to sleep.

The night was quite cold and Jake replenished the fire often, blankets adequate for one were little help divided in two.

Somewhere between midnight and dawn, Jake began to drowse when suddenly the mule moaned softly, pointing his ears toward the opening of the ravine. Getting to his feet Jake moved quickly to position himself between the boulders where he could watch down the ravine yet not be seen by the firelight.

He heard footsteps and the dim figure of a man approached. He watched as the man stole quietly around the rocks and loomed over the girl. There was a flash of firelight on steel as he raised his arm bearing a knife over his head. Jake aimed and pulled the trigger. Bam! The man crumpled to the ground. The girl rose up screaming and ran to Jake to throw her arms around him, only to reel back in repulsion. The first action startled Jake, the second he was used to.

Walking over to the mule, he fumbled in his pack for the one spare wool shirt and gave it to the girl, picked up the blankets, snuffed out the fire and once in darkness, spoke. "Put on that shirt and let's get outta here. We're safer traveling than sleeping. Who are you and what are you doing out here anyway?"

Putting on the shirt and striking off down the trail behind Jake, she replied, "My name is Ruth, and that's all you're going to know about that. As to how I got here, well, that's a rather long story and I'm not too sure you're all that interested. Most all you men are only interested in one thing where a woman is concerned."

Jake stopped. "Now, listen here, young woman, I don't ordinarily run around shooting men for some bawdy house female. You didn't seem to be that kind of woman as far as I could see, but I'm beginning to wonder if the smartest thing for me to have done would have been to let that knife bearing fella finish his work."

Ruth was taken aback. Jake knew it was too dark for her to see his mouth clearly and he mumbled everything so badly, she probably couldn't understand much of what he said.

"Now, I asked you a decent question and it would be nice if you gave me a decent answer." He turned and started walking again.

Stumbling along after him, Ruth, all the sassiness gone out of her voice, went on with her story. "It seems a million years ago that Ma, Pa, my two brothers and myself, left Missouri as a part of a small wagon train. I don't remember how many days out we were, or for that matter how many weeks either, when we were attacked by Indians. It was a terrible and bloody massacre and all were killed except the young girls. There were twelve, none of us over fifteen years old, that were hustled off to a nearby camp. I was thirteen at the time.

"The camp was full of white men and Indians alike. We were put into a large tent to await a rough looking man who checked us over. Stripping us down to our bare skins, he walked back and forth rubbing his tobacco stained chin with a dirty hand. Then separated us according to how developed our figures were. Those of us who were slow developing our women's figures were turned over to the Indians to be used as slaves or killed. The rest of us were handed over to the gang who raped us repeatedly during the night. You could hear the girls crying and pleading to be left alone. I was so scared and I

31

couldn't stop crying. Along about dawn we were loaded into a covered wagon and along with twenty girls in other wagons, headed west.

"Some of the girls starved themselves to death, others became pregnant and were shot. The rest of us were headed to the mining camps as prostitutes.

"I was brought to Bodie and sold to Rosie Mae's Rompers as one of the girls. There are a lot of really bad men that come to Bodie and one of them, they call him 'Duke,' thinks I'm his private property. Well, I'm not, but he's killed more than one man who's taken a liking to me. He won't let anyone near me. That's all right with me. I'm not that kind of girl. I hate it there."

"Well, if you're not that kind of girl, why don't you get out? In fact, how come you didn't leave before now? No one was stopping you."

"Oh yes, there was," blazed Ruth, "that Duke, he always had someone watching me. It was only when he was out of town that I could have some freedom of sorts. He paid Rosie to keep an eye on me, and he paid her plenty."

Ruth paused, sighing. "The other girls in Rosie's like that kind of work, most of them came there on their own. They don't like me much, they say I give the place a bad reputation. But Rosie is afraid of Duke too, and she won't let me go. Not long ago a man and his son came into town on some kind of land deal. I met them at the drug and general merchandise store. The son, Frank, said he wanted to see more of me, even if I was one of Rosie's girls.

"One day when Duke was out of town, I ran some errands for Rosie. Again at the drug store I met Frank. I suggested he meet me that night at six. Ducking Rosie was always hard but I managed. He would come as a customer asking for Betty, who helped me with all this. I think she did it just to get rid of me. We then would go to my room and spend nights planning my escape. Well, Duke came back the very night we sneaked out of town, this very night. I guess he found out real fast I was gone. I didn't even have time to change my clothes or pack. We just took off and ran. They caught up with us and there was a terrible fight, a shot, and Frank is dead. I just ran and ran. I found this ravine and when I heard you coming I thought you was one of Duke's men. Anyhow, that's my story and now I don't know what I'm going to do."

The story made Jake's skin crawl. She couldn't be more than fifteen now. He had not had time to get a really good look at her before dark and he still could not see her well. Fear welled up in his breast as he imagined a man lurking behind every rock and bush. With that load of gold in his mouth, he sure didn't need anything to draw attention to himself. What in hell was he going to do with her?

He watched her stumbling along beside the mule in shoes totally inadequate for fast rough travel and wondered if there was any way she could be added to the mule's burden. By early morning they had reached the first slopes of the Sierras and vegetation became thicker. Locating a spot set high enough for a good lookout, he headed up. Reaching the area he stopped and Ruth dropped gratefully to the ground. The sun was already up and he built a small fire, fixed coffee, some meager food, and the two of them ate in silence.

Ruth finished her meal and sat watching Jake's hunched back. The only thing he seemed to be able to eat was biscuits dunked in coffee and between the sight and the sound, he presented a disgusting picture. She felt pity welling up within her for this unfortunate man.

Jake finished what little food he could force between those terrible teeth. He found the coffee had to be almost stone cold before he could drink it because the heat spread through his mouth, burning his gums and throat.

Ruth helped clean camp and Jake fixed a place for her to lie down. They were both tired and eye weary. Jake sat back and as Ruth prepared herself for rest, he had a good opportunity to observe her.

She did not look her fifteen years of age. There were deep dark circles beneath her eyes, the paint and powder they wore in those houses was dirty and streaked, giving a false impression of wrinkles. Her hair was the color of sage honey and very long. She was small and in Jake's oversized shirt, her breasts, though voluptuous as Jake knew, hardly showed. The quick easy way she handled herself told of her youth but from the side she looked older than her age. The blue eyes still held an underlying innocence, although overshadowed by the brutal life she had been forced to live. Jake sighed, pulled his hat down over his eyes and drowsed in the sun with an ear cocked to the approaching trail. The sun scooted behind clouds and a small breeze began to whisper through the sparse underbrush. Both slept.

Jake awoke with a start. The day had grown colder and darker with clouds forming over the hills. He woke Ruth and leaving some of the food supplies behind, repacked the mule to accommodate Ruth. Now they could make better time.

They traveled all the rest of the day and most of the night. Early morning found them in the desert again with Carson City not too far ahead. The sun was low over the Sierras when they pulled into the outskirts of town. Only then did Jake feel the tension ease over his shoulders. He glanced back at the dismal figure of Ruth weaving on the back of the mule, wondering once again what the hell he was going to do with her. He rotated his head, his neck ached from casting a wary eye over his shoulder all day and his jaw was giving him fits. Shielding his eyes with his hand, he gazed into the distance, he was getting closer now.

CHAPTER SIX

JAKE HAD BEEN to Carson City several times in his wanderings. Having taken refuge with a band of Mormon people headed for Utah, he spread out from there, crisscrossing the west and mid-west until he caught up with the gold migration. One of the families he became well acquainted with was the Garretts. Fred and his wife, Sarah, owned and operated a large ranch just south of the town proper, until Fred became crippled with rheumatism and could hardly get around. Sarah rented rooms in the big house and bunkhouse to help augment their livelihood. Jake had always rented a room there while in Carson City. Both old people had taken a great liking to the deformed man and treated him as no one ever had.

As he entered the yard with Ruth on the mule, Sarah came walking down to meet him. "Good land, boy, what are ya doin' with that young girl? Are ya crazy?" Then spying his bandaged head, said, "You're hurt. Tooth? Jaw? Ya look so funny. Cain't ya answer me, boy?"

With that, Jake removed the rag, put his hands to his mouth

and gratefully spit out his gold teeth. "No, Sarah, I ain't hurt or sick or nothin'. Just was the only way I could think of to get my gold outta town without being killed. As for the girl, I found her along the way. She needs some taking care of and I knew of no one but you we could turn to for help. I'll tell you more about her later, right now she needs attention."

Half asleep, Ruth slid from the mule and with Sarah's help, went into the house. Jake led the mule around back to the bunkhouse. There he unpacked the mule, gave him a much deserved rubdown and turned him loose in the corral. He turned to the bunkhouse and fell into a bed where he slept until morning.

The sun was just slipping up over the eastern edge of the desert as Jake awoke. He cleaned up as best he could and headed to the house for first breakfast call. He was greeted by Fred Garrett. "Howdy, Jake, sure glad ta see ya, son. Say, what the hell happened to yer mouth?"

Jake shook the old man's hand and sat down beside him. Unable to do more than mouth his food on bruised gums and too embarrassed to do so in front of the hired hands and the old couple, he accepted only coffee. "Tell ya all about it after breakfast, Fred."

The men ate and cleared away from the table. Sarah fixed some eggs and told Jake she didn't care what he looked like, just clean up the plate.

Jake gave her a toothless grin and dug in. His first question upon finishing was, "Where's Ruth?"

"Well now, that poor child is still dead asleep. Jake, she's just a young girl, what happened?"

Jake leaned back and told them the whole story, about the gold teeth, and why, about finding Ruth plus the story she told him.

"And now, Sarah, do you suppose you could keep her on here? I would be glad to pay for her keep. Maybe she could help around the house some."

"Don't ya worry about that, son, she's welcome to stay here as long as she cares to." Sarah picked up the dishes as she spoke. Jake got up and helped her clear the table and wipe the dishes.

"Say, Jake," Fred said, "there's a fella in town they say can make store bought teeth that ya cain't tell them from yer own. Whyn't ya go talk ta the feller, see what he can do fer ya?"

"Think I will, Fred, and while I'm at it, I'll take Sarah with me. Ruth needs things and I don't know anything about what women wear."

Sarah quickly agreed to go with him.

"I'll be ready directly," Jake said as he headed for the bunkhouse. There were no more clean shirts so he had to make do with what he had on.

Packing his gold teeth in the bandage worn around his head, he stuck them into his jacket pocket and turned toward the barn. He hitched Fred's two mares to the wagon and led the team up to the back hitching rail. Jake glanced up at the large old house. It needed paint but still showed the grace and dignity of the grand old house it had once been.

Fred Garrett had, at one time, a large spread of cattle. When Carson City began to grow, he sold off parcels of land to the town. About mid-life he became mysteriously ill. The illness panicked him and he spent all of his fortune running to doctors from coast to coast. Employees and rustlers ran off with most of his prize stock, leaving him with a few head of feeder cattle. What was left of his land was planted in alfalfa. Rheumatism set in and he became house bound. The couple had no children and were exceptionally devoted to each other. Jake wondered what old Fred would do if Sarah died first. It would certainly be a tragedy.

The back door swung open and Sarah came out. Jake helped her into the wagon and they headed for town. "Jake, that girl is still sleepin'. I reckon she'll sleep most of the day. It makes my old heart sore to think of that baby, and she's still a baby, and what she's already lived through."

Jake agreed as he pulled up to the general store. Getting down, Sarah said, "Now, I'll be quite a while, Jake, need a few things fer myself and I figure since ya had the wagon hitched, I'd just pick up a few of them. When I'm through I'll be over at Bonnie's Kitchen. Her and me are top friends so don't worry about keepin' me waitin'."

Jake's next stop was the Wells Fargo office where they weighed out his gold teeth. Everyone in the office gathered around to see and finger the gold teeth. Poor Jake became highly embarrassed as laughter rolled around the room. He hoped that news of his teeth would not arrive in Bodie before he did or he might never be able to pull that trick again.

After the laughter died down and the weighing was complete, Jake found himself $4,000 richer. Pretty good money for false teeth, he chuckled.

As Jake turned to take his money to the new accounts department, he nearly stumbled over a man dressed from head to toe in gray.

The gentleman stepped back, gave Jake a sickly smile and dusting himself off with impeccably clean white gloves, spoke. "Quite a haul there and certainly an ingenious method of transporting your gold to town. Do you do that sort of thing often?"

Jake sidestepped the man, gave him a withering look and proceeded on with his business. While filling out his signature card Jake watched the man in gray out of the corner of his eye. He had walked over to two rather ominous looking characters lounging against the far wall of the office, stopped to speak with them, then walked on out of the bank.

Jake watched the incident with curiosity and turning to the clerk asked, "Say, what do you know about that gentleman over there? The one all dressed in gray, like he was going to a funeral?"

The clerk looked, then smiled. "You've about got him pegged right. That's Mr. Lord, our one and only undertaker. Folks here don't care for him much. He seems to acquire a great deal of knowledge about everyone's business. Like a bad vision, he shows up where and when least expected, or for that matter, wanted. How he manages to find out these things I have no idea. Also the company he keeps certainly does not go with the image he presents, like those two rough looking men he was talking to. They are his constant companions. For a funeral, they all get dressed in black and drive the hearse. They act as pallbearers, ushers and anything else that's needed at the service. There are rumors he heads a powerful gang of murdering, robbing cutthroats. No one has ever been able to prove a thing and it hardly seems likely they ever will. You never see him dressed in anything other than gray, spotlessly clean like he just stepped out of the bathtub. Not the type to run a gang but then, you never know. He has this obsession with cleanliness. Has those two clear a path through so he won't have to come in contact with anyone."

"Where does he hail from? Does he come from around here?"

"No one seems to know where he comes from. He just appeared here about a year ago, set himself up in the undertaking business, and with the exception of a weekend or two out of town every month, he is always here. Like it or not, he has become a permanent part of our community. He doesn't seem to have any close friends besides those two bodyguards. He's a total mystery to us all."

"He sure gives me the creeps," Jake said.

Jake opened up a savings account and kept out $1,000 to spend. From there he walked the streets until he found the dentist Fred told him about. The dentist measured and fitted and talked continuously. After some time, he said, "Well, looks like none of the ready made ones I have on hand will do. I'm going to have to make you a special set. Now, that will take a week and because they are a special make, will cost you $75."

Jake gave him a toothless smile and said, "That will be just fine."

Walking out of the dentist office he stopped and glanced up and down the street. Directly across from the dentist office was a sign, LORDS FUNERAL PARLOR, COME, TALK TO THE LORD, A WIDOWS BEST FRIEND. Jake had to chuckle, what a name for an undertaker.

CHAPTER SEVEN

TURNING THE WAGON around, Jake headed north toward the stables. As he approached the corrals, a young boy came out of the mule sheds. He limped as he walked and Jake noticed that one foot was crippled. The boy spotted Jake, stopped and stared. Then setting down the bucket he was carrying, spoke. "Can I help ya, mister?"

"Maybe. Do you work here?"

"Yeah, my name's Paul and I help around the barns and stables. Are ya lookin' fer somethin' special?"

"Yes, mules I think."

"Sure, right over there," he gestured, "at the feedin' trough." Turning, he led Jake over to where several mules and perhaps a dozen burros were feeding. Jake wondered if he should buy one of those stubborn little animals. Many of the miners used them. *Well, I don't know*, mused Jake. *They seem so small and they would be slower than a mule*. He looked the mules over, not too good a selection to choose from, he figured.

"Lookin' fer somethin' special?" asked Paul.

41

"Well, something at least better than what you have here."

Paul beckoned with his finger and led Jake around the corner. There Jake saw two of the most beautiful mules he had ever seen anywhere in his life. They were red in color and big as a good-sized horse. They turned their heads to look at him as he approached. One had a white blaze on his face, the other was pure red with white tipped hairs, giving him a frosted look. Jake walked around them, feeling their legs, looking into their mouths, checking their teeth and eyes. My, they were a grand pair. Yes, sir, he wanted those mules. "How come they're hidden back here outta sight?"

"I put them here," Paul said. "I didn't want just anyone to buy them. They're different than the rest, real different. I wanted someone to buy them that would love them, that's what they need, lots of love. Especially that one with the white forehead, he's a real baby."

"Where'd they come from, Paul?"

"Don't rightly know, mister...er, I don't think I got yer name?"

"Just call me Jake, Paul."

"Well, anyway, one mornin' I showed up fer work and they were in the corral. When I went to feed them, they made over me so much that I knew right away they were special." Paul took Jake over to the blacksmith shed. "There, the blacky is the owner of all the stock and equipment around here. I'll just go get them ready fer ya."

"Thank you, Paul." Jake walked into the shed, found the blacksmith and paid him for the mules. He tied them to the back of the wagon and found them to be extremely balky. The poor mares were hard put to drag the two big stubborn mules through town. Jake wondered if he wouldn't have been better off with two stubborn burros. They would have been easier for the mares to drag. Perhaps he had made a mistake, listening to Paul. Maybe the boy made him soft in the head because of the similarity of their conditions.

He dragged the mules up to Bonnie's Kitchen where he met Sarah and had a light lunch. The next stop was the general store to pick up the supplies.

"My Gawd, Sarah, did you buy out the whole store?"

"Relax, boy, some of that is fer the house."

Jake laughed and went in to pay the bill. Sarah followed him in, calling, "Jake, Jake, wait, only the stuff fer Ruth is what yer payin' fer."

"Now, Sarah, how many times have you and Fred bunked me and fed me for free? Now it's my turn to help and I'm gonna' do it."

They returned home early afternoon. Jake untied the dragging mules and put them in the corral with his other mule. He then unloaded the wagon and helped Sarah carry the things for Ruth upstairs. At the door he paused as Sarah tapped gently and called, "Ruth, Ruth honey, are ya awake?" No answer, and turning the knob slowly, she opened the door and they went in.

Ruth lay still in slumber. Jake looked at her sleeping form. He trembled and a wave of tenderness flowed through his body. To him she was the most beautiful thing he had ever seen. He put down the packages softly and bent over her. Taking a shaking hand, he drew her hair out of her eyes and face. Lord, how lovely and how young she was.

He was suddenly, and for the first time, filled with pain and dismay at the fate life had dealt him. Without his crooked back, and if he was a few years younger, he would gladly have fought dragons for her love. As he stood up to leave, a tear fell from his cheek onto her pillow. He wiped his eyes, he had not been aware of crying.

Sarah stood by watching with tears in her own eyes. Oh, if only the young thing could know of the warmth and beauty of that tortured man's soul, surely his twisted back would mean nothing and she would learn to love him. Sarah would try. Yes, she would try. Together they walked out of the room and closed the door.

Jake stopped Sarah in the kitchen, saying, "I think I had better disappear for a while. I really do not want to be around when Ruth wakes up. The dentist said my teeth would be ready in a week and I want to try out these two mules I bought. So I'm going to pack up into the mountains for a week." He kissed Sarah on the cheek, said good-bye to Fred, and went to pack the mules and leave.

Oddly enough, the two animals worked well together now that they were not being insulted by having to follow a wagon, and struck off down the road.

As he began his ascent up into the low-lying hills, he had a prickly feeling he was being followed. *Now, who in hell would be following me?* Jake thought. *I don't have a thing that anyone would be interested in at this point.* He tied the mules and crept back to a spot where he could view the trail. Sure enough, two horsemen were tracking him. *Now, what the hell…well, I'll be Gawd damn, it's those two bodyguards of Mr. Lord's. Now just what the hell are they following me for? Maybe they're going to shoot me. Could be that's how Mr. Lord gets his business, then again perhaps that rumor was right and the impeccable Mr. Lord is all tied up with some gang. Even if that was true, it still didn't make any sense that they would follow me.* Then the conversation he had with Mr. Lord at the bank counter struck him: "Certainly an ingenious method of transporting your gold to town. Do you do that sort of thing often?" *So that's what they're looking for, well, by Gawd, we'll just have to give them a run for their money.*

Going back to the mules and chuckling to himself, he began leading the two horsemen a merry chase. This lent adventure to an otherwise boring trip. Many exhausting days later, Jake stopped on top of an overhanging ledge and looked back down at the two horsemen struggling up an impossible trail. He was sure they were as tired of trying to figure out what he was going to do next, as he was trying to confuse them. Think I'll give this up, I've been up here a week now and I'm ready to go back. The two horsemen, realizing they were being led in circles, gave up and disappeared.

CHAPTER EIGHT

HE CAME DOWN out of the mountains into Carson City, stopped at the dentist, had his teeth fitted, paid the man and left. As he passed store windows, he would stop and smile at his reflection. *Hmm*! mused Jake. *Not bad lookin'. No, sir, not bad lookin' at all.*

He led the mules to the general store where he purchased new flannel shirts and jeans, a pack of new underwear and a pair of boots. He next headed for the gun counter. There were several nice rifles but the one that caught his eye was a .52 caliber Spencer. He asked the young man behind the counter if he could look at it along with a Winchester Trapper Model. Jake hefted each one to his shoulder and sighted down the barrel. The Winchester felt good but he disliked the octagonal barrel. Jake pivoted and swung the rifle into firing position. Hmm! Not bad, but not good either. He then picked up the Spencer .52 and repeated the action. "Now, that's more like it," he spoke to the young man. "What do you have in the way of a good pistol?"

"Right over here, sir," the clerk spoke excitedly, "we have a new pistol that just came in last week. It was made in 1875 but we just got it out here. It's a new Colt .44 single action, rim fire." He handed the pistol to Jake.

"Now, that's a pistol," said Jake as he caressed it, fitted it into the palm of his hand, cocked and sighted down the long 7½ inch barrel. "Yes, sir, that's a pistol. Now, I would say that these two pieces of firearms would be just about all a fellow would need. Now I will also need about two cartons of shells for this nice new pistol, and about four of the shells for the Spencer."

"Yes, sir, will there be anything else?" The clerk eyed Jake's condition wondering what he needed all these firearms for. Perhaps to defend himself against those who would take advantage of him?

"Well, yes, I forgot long johns, and I would like to see two of those heavy plaid wool jackets, also a couple pairs of high top laced boots. Let's see, how about three of those wool blankets, and hats, I need at least two felt hats." While Jake was trying on the boots, he spied a table full of trousers. "Oh, by the way, better give me four of those trousers also."

He stood up and the clerk measured him asking, "What color do you want?"

"Oh, let's see, give me two dark blue and two brown."

"Yes, sir, now will that be all?"

Jake gave the clerk a big grin, saying, "Yes, I guess so. Say, there isn't a barbershop around close, is there?"

"One block down, next to the bath house."

Jake split two loads between the mules and led them down to the barbershop where he had a haircut and beard trim. If you looked at him straight on he was very presentable. His hunched back made him quite short but he carried himself well. Getting all spiffed up for what? He felt a tingle in his spine. Did he think Ruth would be interested in him if he were cleaned up?

She hadn't really seen him without his dirty bandage and bushy hair.

He next stopped at the food store where he ordered several sacks of flour, salt, sugar, beans, coffee and corn meal. He told the owner to fix it up and he would be back later to pick it up and pay for the order.

Having picked up his supplies he went back to the ranch where he unpacked his animals and broke out a new shirt, pants and a pair of his new boots. Washed and dressed, hair combed and store bought teeth shining at him in the mirror, he figured he looked mighty fine. As he turned to go up to the house, he glanced at himself sideways and shuddered. If only he didn't have that awful deformed body!

He walked up to the house and entered the back door. Sarah was preparing the evening meal and Ruth was helping. Jake's heart did flips as he watched the girl. She was dressed in blue and her golden hair was caught behind and tied with a big blue bow. Jake knew he would have to leave for Bodie soon or he would never go.

Sarah turned. "Lord, boy, ya look so fine. Was thinkin' ya had gone on back without sayin' good-bye."

Ruth looked back over her shoulder and eyes widened. All she had ever seen of Jake was a hunched, bandaged, bundled, wild-eyed, bushy haired man. Why, his face was beautiful and his eyes were not wild but intense, filled with compassion, pain and yes, passion. "Oh, Jake, how good you look. And look at me." She pivoted around for him. "I love all the new things you bought for me. And five bolts of material for more dresses. You shouldn't have spent so much money on me."

Was this the woman he had found in the ravine, this young girl with her golden hair cascading to her waist, and her cheeks pink with pleasure? The only thing womanly about her was her ample breasts straining at the top of her dress. Jake stared.

Suddenly they were both stricken with shyness as she

became aware of his eyes on her bosom. They were complete strangers. Neither one the same person that had traveled that strenuous trail across the desert. Ruth turned and with flaming cheeks fled, while Jake retired to the bunkhouse.

The trip home was cold and tiresome. Jake's heart was not in the going but he knew he had made the right decision. The three mules worked well together and Jake found room to ride the small mule part of the way.

He labored on, head bent against the wind and mind drifting. He had never before been lonesome but the thought of that lonely stone hut made him shudder. So while he was in Carson City he wired his old friend, Cad Mercer, and invited him to join him in Bodie. He knew Cad was ill and that he might not make it if he did come, but he sure hoped he would. The clouds were beginning to blow in from the mountains and the air turned bitterly cold. Jake was afraid he would never make Bodie. Night fell and found him without much in the way of a shelter. He put nosebags on the mules, tied them together, hobbled, still packed. He then rummaged around for some food for himself, wrapped up in several blankets and lay down to rest. Several hours before dawn he awoke to a drizzling rain. He got up, unpacked an oil slicker, tied up his blankets, took the hobbles off the mules and headed for Bodie. It was smarter to keep going than lie there and freeze to death.

Far back and unbeknown to Jake, two horsemen, heads bent against the wind and rain, were following Jake's trail.

The trip home took him half a day less than going to Carson City due to the absence of Ruth. It was dark when he pulled into the outskirts of Bodie and he headed straight for Pete's place. There he stayed the night telling them all of his adventures in Carson City. It was late when they retired. The countryside was quiet, clouds lowered down and blanketed the sinful town from the rest of the world.

CHAPTER NINE

CADWELL MERCER READ and reread the telegram. He and Jake had kept their friendship going for many years. They seldom saw each other and only when Jake happened to be near a town did he catch up with Cad's letters. Now Jake was inviting him out to Bodie to join him in his search for gold.

Cad thought about it all day and most of the night. Life here was miserable. His singing career was ruined by the advent of consumption. He coughed all the time and had spells of bloodletting from his lungs. There was no one left in his family to care for and no one to care for him. If he were going to die, he would rather die with a friend than alone in this damn town. He turned over the house to a distant shirttail cousin and her family, sold what he could, gave away the rest and began setting in certain stores he knew he would never be able to buy out there.

He knew nothing of the climate but figured anything in the desert would be hot. By the time all plans were set it was January 1878. He boarded the train for Arizona where he would pick up another train to Reno, Nevada. He could buy clothes and pack animals there and head for Bodie.

He was shocked to find snow on the ground at Reno. The people had tried to tell him weather and travel was worse farther out but he wouldn't believe them and struck off by himself. He really had no idea which way to go and the map the stationmaster had drawn for him was sketchy, to say the least. He had purchased a compass before he left home but was not very adept at using it.

What would have normally taken four and a half days took him ten. He lost his horse, had a bad coughing spell which left him weak and by the time he hit Bodie, blood was running from his mouth and freezing on his stubby beard. Bitter cold winds raged across the top of the hills and tumbled down the canyons and ravines, carrying with it a blind of snow. Cad could feel the mules quicken their stride, and reaching up, he grabbed the pack strap of each animal allowing them to drag him the last few feet. Through the murky darkness could be seen the light from a small rock shack, and as he fell to the ground, he could hear the soft sounds of harmonica music from within. Giving a rasping cough, blood spewing from his mouth, he lapsed into darkness.

Jake Stone placed his harmonica on the table beside him. Surely that was more than the devil wind he heard. Pulling himself to his feet, he hunched his way toward the door. In the lantern glow, with his dark hair and beard falling in an unkempt manner about his head and face, he looked like a wild man. He reached for his gun as he approached the door. Cautiously he opened it, viewing the sprawled man on the snow. "My God, Cad, you made it!" He flung open the door and pulled the unconscious man into the warmth of the room.

Slowly, Cad resumed consciousness. The first thing he was aware of was the howling of that terrible wind, then the warmth of sheepskin bundled around him. The sounds of pans rattling, mules munching hay, boiling coffee sending out a heavenly aroma, and Jake's voice humming.

"Cad. By Gawd, Cad, I believe you're gonna make it. If you don't spew out your lungs first, you'll make it." Cad rolled his head to one side, tears of relief dimmed his eyes and sleep overtook him once again.

As Jake stoked the fire, he looked over at his sleeping friend wondering if he had done the right thing, inviting him here. Just getting here almost killed him and staying here in Bodie surely would. The temperature this very day was between 30 and 40 degrees below zero, and the never ceasing wind almost a hundred miles an hour. Jake sat back, lit his pipe, and staring into the coals allowed his mind to drift.

It was summer in Philadelphia and he was down by the river fishing. In the distance he could hear the sound of someone singing. The singing grew louder and from behind the bend a small boat bearing a young boy drifted into view. Spying Jake, he stopped singing and waved. Jake's first thought was one of panic, should he run before his crooked body could be seen or take a chance on being ridiculed once again. Something in the smile of the boy kept him from running. As the boy beached the boat, he spoke. "Hello, my name is Cad Mercer. What's yours?"

Jake scowled from beneath his heavy black brows and mumbled, "Jake Stone," and slowly reeled in his line. He watched as the boy dropped himself down on the grassy bank beside him. There was no sign of shock or repulsion as the boy glanced at his back.

"Say, do the kids give you a bad time about your back?"

"Yeah," replied Jake.

"Well, it looks like we're two of a kind then," said the boy. "I've been sick most of my life and music is a passion with me. I hope to sing opera and be on the stage some day, and because I'm always so skinny and sickly, they call me a sissy."

Jake took a long look at the boy, then smiled and a warm closeness was formed between the two.

A rasping cough brought Jake back to the present and he glanced over at the sleeping man. Some twenty odd years had passed since that bright summer day. Twenty-eight years and Cad was still a sickly frail man, never reaching his life ambition as an opera singer. He refused to quit singing for benefits even after contracting consumption. Freely he gave of his marvelous voice and now he was out here on the desert to heal or die, and from the looks of him, it would be the latter.

Jake picked up the pot of heated herbs and oils he was preparing and went over to Cad and opening his shirt, began rubbing it into his chest until the flesh turned red. Then he rolled him over and did the same on his back. Taking the shirt, he walked over to the pot of melted sheep fat, dumped it in, soaked it, then putting the greasy mess back on, wrapped him mummy-like with several of Cad's blankets. There Cad was to stay, being hand-fed mutton stew, for several weeks.

Cad awoke with the strong odor of rotted flesh or dead sheep and rotted foliage, or...what the hell was that damn smell anyway? His eyes flew open and memory began to return. He looked down at himself wrapped tightly in blankets and tried to move. As he did so, the warm air from his body floated up into his nostrils and he almost vomited. That damnable odor is coming from ME!

Weeks of herbs and oils and melted sheep fat, sweat and dirt created a smell the devil himself would not allow around the gates of hell. He glanced around the room to find himself alone. "JAKE? GODDAMNIT, JAKE, WHERE THE HELL ARE YOU?" he bellowed. "Get me out of this grease soaked outhouse before I die from my own fumes!"

No answer. Cad's eyes wandered around the room. Jake had written and described the town, the fabulous amounts of gold that was being taken out of the hills, but he failed to explain his own humble existence. Cad surveyed the room. The floor was sloped gently and was trenched along the back and side to allow water to drain. There were gold pans stacked against the wall, the furniture was made of planks and scrap wood and stays from wooden barrels. The chairs were pickle barrels cut halfway down and halfway through. The lid was then placed over the center for a seat. The backs were strapped, leaving them curved to fit your back. The hut was bleak and damp. Water ran from the walls as the heat from the fireplace met the icy stone. It surprised Cad at the warmth of the air inside. He wondered if he would be able to live in surroundings like this. It certainly was a far cry from the sterile life he led in Philadelphia.

One of the mules set up a rusty bray as Jake hunched his way through the door. Pleasure and relief showed in Jake's eyes as he looked at his friend. Cad boomed, "Come on, Jake, get me out of this smelly mess."

Jake grinned, walked over to the hearth and laid down his snow-covered wood. "Sure thing, you rotten smelling lark. I'm kind of interested to see what you look like under that stuff."

"How about a bath?"

"Bath?" Jake snorted. "Man, you gotta be out of your mind! Nobody takes a bath out here in the wintertime, least of all you." With that he reached over and put a large pot of sheep fat over the blaze. Then he walked over to Cad and began to unwrap him. "Phew! You sure are ripe, all right."

Cad's skin beneath all the herbal oils was peeling off in great patches. Jake took a rag and wiped off all the dead skin and rancid fat. Then dipping a new shirt in the pot of melted fat, placed it back on Cad, finishing him off in a clean wool shirt over the fat soaked one.

In this manner, the winter months moved on. Cad grew healthier and fatter. His flesh filled out until he no longer had need for Jake's home remedies.

Early spring brought the warm sun. So warm, the snows melted and ran great rivers of water down the hillside and the dry creeks ran over their banks taking with them tents and lean-tos carelessly built on their sides. This did not seem to bother the miners and much frantic panning took place. Even the trenches in Jake's hut overran its banks and almost flooded them out. Fast melting snows caused the hill to crumble into the room and they had to rapidly shovel mud out the front door. In so doing, they came across a sizeable vein of rich color. Jake stopped and gaped, mouth open, watching water and mud flow across rich quartz. He threw his arms in the air, dancing around and shouting like a madman.

"God damn, my own house! Hee! Hee! Hee! My own God damn house. All this time and I been setting right on top of the stuff."

He twirled and pivoted, losing his balance, and fell headlong into the mud and water where he splashed happily, and in the residue of mud that ran from his beard could be seen the sparkle of gold dust as it clung to the hairs.

CHAPTER TEN

JAKE AND CAD did not go into Bodie to stake their claim. They figured that the less anyone knew of their find, the better off they would be. After all, the hut was rightfully Jake's, and also the land it was built upon. And besides, who would suspect a mine right inside their own house?

Jake reached for the coffee pot and poured a cup for Cad and one for himself, saying, "If we take small amounts of ore into Bodie to sell, it would be noticed that we were doing some mining. At least clearing enough ore to make a small living. It would keep the mine jumpers off our back. What do you think?"

"You would know better than I," replied Cad.

"You know, Cad, it's been some time since I showed myself in Bodie. I wonder if there is anyone there that even remembers me? Why don't we ride on over and let me show you the town. I probably wouldn't recognize it myself. I understand from Pete that the town has grown like a mushroom patch."

"I'd like that, Jake, thought for a time there you brought me all the way out here just to keep me cooped up in this rock house of yours."

Jake only owned one saddle, so he put it on Moonshine for Cad. He could ride old Blaze bareback. He would pick up another saddle in Bodie.

"All set, Cad?"

"All set. Let's ride in and rip her wide open. I'm just raring for some fun."

With the new road to town, the time it took to ride there was shortened by half an hour. So, for a little under half an hour, they could ride from the hut to Bodie.

Jake was flabbergasted when they crested the hill. The town was a booming city. You could hear dance hall music clear up here on the hill. The voices and laughter from them all rang from the hillsides.

Cad was fairly shivering with excitement. Jake had never seen him like this before. *Sure as hell hope he doesn't go off his head over this*, mused Jake. *I know that gold and the feverish gambling and the hell raising it creates, is quite often the downfall of many a man in the gold fields.*

They rode on down Main Street and turned right on Green. Jake then took him up Wood Street to the Bunker Hill Mine and Mill, which was now the Standard Mine and Mill. Jake wondered when that took place. He was sure out of step with the rest of the world. They circled around and came back on Main again. Tying the mules, Cad and Jake strode off on foot. Gambling halls and prostitutes were thick as fleas. Gunmen lurked outside every saloon and one never knew for sure whom he was talking to.

Cad was enthralled with the sights and sounds of Bodie and began a complete tour of every store and business house up and down the street, while Jake purchased a saddle and put it on Blaze.

He and Cad drank and gambled in every saloon and

gambling hall they came to. Cad seemed to be incredibly lucky, for they came away with far more than they went in with. There didn't seem to be anyone except a few miners who remembered Jake, and he was having the time of his life. They became so drunk that they hit one of the local bawdy houses.

"Gawd damn it, Cad, why did you let me go in one of those filthy places? I know better but I guess I'm just drunk enough to think I could get away with it. Those cheap females, why do they think they're so good that they can make fun of my back? Let's go get another drink. I feel all sobered up again. Cheap dirty bitches, never again! Tramps, all of them, tramps." He thought of Ruth, how could she ever have been caught up in that slime pit? His heart warmed at the thought of her, remembering her soft white bosom and long golden hair.

It was early morning when the two of them rode back to the hut. Another hour would see the sun breaking over the top of the hill. They slid off the mules, unsaddled them and turned both animals loose, then fell into their bunks and into a duet of loud snoring slumber.

Jake sat nursing a cup of strong black coffee, trying to remember what he had done and why. One thing he did remember was talking to a Mr. Soderling in one of the saloons about the use of cyanide in extracting gold from quartz. Jake had heard of the process briefly while in Utah but had never pursued it. He was only doing small bits of panning at the time, just enough to buy a little food or clothing.

"I wonder, Cad, if we could learn to use that cyanide without killing ourselves? I hear it's powerful stuff but I really don't know how it works."

"Well, don't look at me," Cad said, yawning, scratching his head and pouring himself a cup of coffee, "and with my lungs you're not going to get me to use it."

"Yeah, that's right too. Guess maybe it's not too good of an idea. I forgot about you and your lung problems."

"Wish I could forget," Cad said, sitting down hard and leaning his elbows on the table. "But I have to admit I do feel better since I have been living out here than I have felt for months."

Jake and Cad worked on their diggings for several weeks. There seemed to be a great deal of gold bearing ore in the center of the hill. Jake worked feverishly but Cad began to slow down considerably. Finally the day came when he felt he could no longer dig in the mine with Jake. He kept thinking of Bodie and all the fun they had while there and he was eager to return. *Well*, thought Jake, *I guess he could go in and bring back a few supplies.*

"If you want, Cad, we'll saddle up old Moonshine and you can go into town and bring back fresh vegetables and a sack of coffee and whatever else strikes your fancy."

"Great," responded Cad, "I'll do just that. It may take awhile though 'cause I'm going to have myself some fun while I'm there."

Jake sighed, well, Cad was a grown man and he could really do as he wished. He noticed that Cad took a small sack of gold with him, which meant he probably wouldn't be back until the wee small hours again. Guess that's all right, too. He wished he had more of the spirit of fun and Cad had more of the spirit of work, that would make them a pretty good team, but then poor Cad did not have Jake's stamina for hard work anyway.

Cad began taking small amounts of gold dust and heading for Bodie daily. He found he could always manage to come home with as much if not more than he took. One night he became so lucky and so drunk, he jumped up on the stage with the dancing girls and began to sing. Bodie had never heard the likes of his booming voice. He sang for hours, rollicking, rough, hard hitting songs that delighted the people and soon the saloon was filled to overflowing with people. Each night, when he hit town, the gambling houses would vie for his presence.

He found he could make more money singing than digging gold with Jake. Also, for him it was much more enjoyable.

This worried Jake to no end for he could smell trouble. Night after night, Cad would make the rounds singing and gambling. He was a handsome man and the women made a great fuss over him. This also forbade trouble and Jake was about to worry himself into a fit over it. He tried to talk to Cad but to no avail.

One night, Jake found Cad propped against his door, out cold, blood running from his head, a note pinned to his chest that read:

KEEP THIS SILLY SON-OF-A-BITCH OUT OF BODIE!

"Silly son-of-a-bitch. Yep, that would really describe Cad all right," Jake said out loud. He grabbed Cad by the coat and dragged him into the house. The wounds to his head were minor and he just let him lay on the floor. Looking at him he could see the toll Cad's nightlife was taking on him.

Cad moaned and rolled over. "Who the hell hit me?" he asked.

"I don't rightly know, Cad, but Gawd damn, it's a wonder you didn't get your fool head blown off. Felt like doing it a time or two myself, here of late. Keep telling you but, no, you're too Gawd damn stubborn. That note pinned to your chest says it about right. You've been acting just like a silly son-of-a-bitch. What is it you want? To get the both of us shot? I didn't ask you out here to go beller'n all over town like a flappy-lipped Romeo. You've been squawkin' and messin' around with those damn dance hall gals 'til you'll end up dyin' of disease at both ends, if some bastard don't blow your stupid damn head off first."

Cad sat there on the floor, still feeling fuzzy headed, with a stupid grin on his face, looking up at Jake. "Aw, come on, Jake, gol dang it. I'd rather die here with my head blown off havin' fun, than in some damn hospital spittin' my lungs out. At least I'm living while I can. Damn, man, you know I'm not long in this world. You might have saved my life but only for a little while. The winters out here are savage. All I need is another cold and I'll be gone before spring and you know it."

Jake just stared at him. Yes, he knew it. He threw up his hands and turned around to find something to clean the blood off Cad's head.

"You know, Cad, I love you like a brother. I guess that's what bothers me so much when I see you doing things like this to yourself. I never was close to my family and I never allowed myself to get too close to anyone to call them good friends. You're the only one that knows me for what I am, not for how I look. The only others close to me is Pete, down there, Ruth and the Garretts. So you'll have to excuse me if I seem overprotective."

He finished wiping the blood off Cad's head and helped him to his bunk. Something was going to have to be done about Cad's nightlife. He just could not go on this way. Jake stood looking down at the sleeping Cad. He acted as if he was still a young boy, almost as if he had never grown up. In a way, Jake felt as if he was raising a son instead of sharing a rough life in the gold fields with a friend. But then, all that did was endear Cad to him all the more.

Jake was awake most of the night trying to figure out a way to entertain Cad at home for a while. It was evident that he was not going to be much help to Jake around the mine. Also, his health had taken a turn for the worse. All the late night gambling and singing, plus the drinking and singing, plus the bawdy-house girls and the singing, was really beginning to show.

Jake pondered, *We could take a trip up into the mountains to do a little panning in the creeks and rivers. If we stayed there long enough, we could also bring home a supply of fresh venison or bear meat for the winter ahead. Yes, that's exactly what we'll do. All I have to do is convince Cad.* Jake sighed as he fell asleep.

Cad sat on the edge of his bunk and yawned, why was it such a crime for him to have a little fun in his life? Jake was beginning to sound like a nagging wife or mother. Now he wanted to pack him off into the mountains to look for more gold. That man was sure obsessed by the color of that yellow metal. He stood up, stretched, yawned again, and shuffled over to the steaming coffee pot. "Tell ya what, Jake, old man, think I'll just skip this little side trip you're planning. You can do better without me anyhow."

"Gawd damn it, Cadwell Mercer, do you think I'm going up into those mountains just to please myself? Whoever wrote that note calling you a silly son-of-a-bitch sure knew what he was talking about. You are undoubtedly the stupidest man I've come in contact with in a long time. I don't remember you as being this unthinking before, what's gotten into you anyway?"

"I don't know, Jake, I really don't know. Why are you dragging me along on your panning trip anyway? I really don't care that much for prospecting and you know it. You know I slow you down, even your crippled body is more useful than I am." Jake was beside himself, how could this man figure that the only thing he was going after was gold.

"Say, Cad, didn't you hear me tell you that we're going on this trip to keep you from getting your head blown off? And besides, that change of altitude would be good for you. There is also the fact that we could use fresh meat for a change, something besides Pete's sheep. There's lots of good big deer and bear up in that country."

Cad stared at Jake and guessed he'd take a walk and think it over. The morning air was already hot and the smell of the sage mingled with smoke from the mesquite fire Jake was using to cook breakfast, began to clear Cad's aching head. He breathed deeply, gazing off across the little valley to the hazy blue-velvet mountains in the distance. Maybe it wouldn't be such a bad idea after all. He could almost feel the cool thin air and smell the pungent odor of pine and fir. Also, it would be good to bathe in the icy waters of some clear stream after months of Jake's old wooden tub. Yes, it would be good for him. Poor Jake, thought Cad, it must be an awful burden on him to have me in his life. I wonder if he would have sent for me if he knew I was going to be so much trouble. Maybe I'd better shape up a bit.

The rest of the day was spent planning what they were going to take on the trip. Along around dusk, Pete came trudging up the hill to the stone hut. Both Cad and Jake had the same idea at the same time. Let's take Pete along with us. They told Pete of their plans for a panning and hunting trip. Pete stood back and eyed them. "What air ya really up to?"

"Well, Pete, it's this way." He showed Pete the note that was pinned to Cad's chest. "If I don't do something about this nut, I'm afraid someone else will."

"Damn it, Cad," laughed Pete, "what the hell did you do now?"

Cad grinned sheepishly and glanced at Jake. "I sorta got myself in trouble in town last night, Pete, and I guess the local yokels got sore about it, so Jake decided we ought to go somewhere and lay low for a spell."

Pete nodded his head. Yes, he knew of Cad's misadventures in the saloons. The man really should have known better, as well educated as he was.

"Wal, fellas, I don't know as if I ought to go off for that long and leave my family. I don't know if they can fend fer themselves. Suppose some of those thievin' bastards come around while I'm gone? Still, I would find it pleasurable after all this heat we've been havin'."

"Come on, Pete, get old man Potter to look in on your family while we're gone. We'll have a hell of a time and get ourselves some meat other than your sheep for a change."

"Let me think on it fer a spell. You all ain't goin' for a while or so, air ya?"

"As soon as possible, Pete."

"I'll go down and talk to the wife about it. See how she takes to the idea."

It was two days later before Pete returned. He had the look of a youngster about to go to his first circus, on his face. He threw his hat in the air, let out a war whoop, and yelled, "Gawd damn it, if'n I cain't go. Yahoo!" He danced around whooping and crowing like a wild man. Jake had never seen so much enthusiasm out of Pete before. Generally he was a quiet calm man. It tickled Jake to see him so.

The great morning finally came for their departure, even Blaze seemed to feel that this was something special and let out a series of rusty brays. Cad even picked up the enthusiasm and was singing along with Blaze's bray. It was bound to be a great trip.

CHAPTER ELEVEN

THE MORNING WAS blistering with a strong hot wind blowing up the red dust from around the mule's feet. "God, I'm glad to be turning my back of this land of the furnaces of hell," said Cad. "It seems there's no happy medium in this country. It's either hotter than hell or colder than hell."

They traveled for three days up into the Sierras. Around noon on the fourth day, they came upon a fast flowing stream. It swept down out of the high hills and into a small meadow surrounded by tall pines and firs. It was a beautiful spot and they decided to make camp there. That night they sat around the campfire and listened to Cad sing ballads of the old west and the mining sorrows of broken dreams.

Next day the trio walked into the hills. The stream seemed to have many bends and crooks to it. Also, a short way up there was another even smaller stream that joined the larger one. It looked like an ideal spot to try some really serious panning. The waters were not running too swiftly or too slow. It was shallow enough to try diverting its course in several places. The idea excited them for it was a different kind of prospecting than they had been doing the past few years.

"Tell us, Jake, how do ya go about this har type of diggin'?" asked Pete.

"Well, I haven't done a whole heap of this type of diggin' myself, but I do know something about it. I spent a summer up in the Utah mountains one year with an old prospector who taught me how to divert a stream at a crook, where the gold piles up against the opposite bank. Then you dig out the soft sand, washing the dust out of each shovel full. When you reach hardpan, you can look for the real big ones. They get caught in the cracks over the years. The small stuff just sorta wanders downstream collecting in the bends as it goes. When you get tired of pannin', you can take to diggin'. Here, let me draw you a picture of how it goes. Then maybe you and Cad can follow what I mean."

Jake drew the course of the little stream as he remembered it, showing how the force of the water would concentrate the path of heavier nuggets to the shortest route downstream. He then pointed out the old alternate streambed that evidently ran with water during the heavy rain season but was dry now. By plugging up the stream at this point and changing most of the water into the dry bed, they could work two inner banks. He explained that the heavier, richer ore, or nuggets, could be found in the cracks and crevices of the bedrock beneath the sand and gravel. By removing the sand and gravel with shovels, they could concentrate on picking and prying up the bedrock and washing the deposits of sand and gravel that had collected there, they should be able to strike some solid color.

Walking back up the stream again they took special note of the bed and of any obstructions that would also catch and hold the larger nuggets. Several large boulders were located a short distance off one of the inner banks that could be worked. This excited Jake and he pointed out how great a "hot spot" this was.

The first job was to cut down some of the saplings with which to make a dam. Cad forgot about his failing health and swung his axe with a vengeance, sweat pouring down his face.

The day wore on with warm sun, cool breezes and a small audience of lizards. A blue jay screeched from overhead proclaiming his disfavor with the noisy disruption of the usual quiet meadow. Blaze stood comfortably at ease in the meadow while his five companions grazed nearby.

After the logs were cut and placed into position, they studied the bottom of the little stream. Pools of water were still caught in the deeper places and a small ripple managed to escape the bonds of the crude dam, laughing its merry way on the original course. There was a great deal of sand and gravel compiled on the inner swing of the bank that would require many hours of back-breaking labor to remove. Undaunted enthusiasm carried them into the job without a thought of the work involved. Darkness, once the sun dipped behind the crest of the mountain, enveloped them rapidly. They dropped their shovels and staggered back to camp, bodies aching with weariness.

"Ouch," moaned Jake, "I didn't think this would be so all fired wearing. Guess I don't remember the work involved in this type of mining." He placed his hands against the small of his back, rocked back and forth moaning, "Oh, Gawd, how I hurt. Guess we shouldn't have tried to do it all in one day. Two would have been better. I see three people with more of a case of gold fever than I thought. I suppose that's why we're still hanging on to Bodie."

Jake dropped back onto his blankets and closed his eyes, experiencing a slight spinning in his head. More than likely he wasn't used to working this hard in high altitude, even his heart was pounding. He opened his eyes and rolled his head to one side to survey the other two. They were sprawled on their blankets, eyes closed, mouths open, snoring loudly. Jake chuckled to himself. Bet the thought of Bodie was the farthest thing from their minds right now. *Good for us all,* mused Jake as he drifted off to sleep.

The wind rose, softly singing in the boughs of the pines, an old hooty owl called to his mate, and the moon began to crest the hill. All these things were lost to the three sleeping men. Even the lack of supper did not seem to bother them.

Morning brought a change in the weather. Clouds scudded across the sky and a chill wind began to blow. *Damn,* thought Jake, *I suppose it's going to rain and wash out our dam, all of our hard work for nothing.* He rolled over in his blankets. *Oh,* he moaned, *stiff, stiff, as if I'd never worked a day in my life.* A good hot cup of coffee was what he needed right now. Hunger pangs snarled through his stomach reminding him that he had not eaten last night.

Taking his toe, he nudged Cad in the back. "All right, you fellas, rise and shine. It's a beautiful day, the sun is gone, the wind has risen and clouds are rolling in over the mountains, and if it don't snow, then it sure as hell gonna rain. And if it rains, then we're right back where we started from. Not only that but we don't have any kind of shelter rigged up for either one, and to top it all off, I'm so Gawd damn hungry I could eat both of you put together. So let's move."

"Looks like our lives are in danger if we don't get that wild man some breakfast," drawled Pete as they all set to work, and before long the aroma of coffee and bacon filled the air. Cad mixed up an enormous batch of flapjacks and the smell of them cooking brought the panhandling Blaze trotting into camp for his share.

The main thing now was to erect some kind of lean-to that would protect them from the weather. They stripped some pine boughs from the lower branches, made poles and used the canvas tarp over all. They had no sooner completed it than a light drizzle started to fall, sour faces all, they sat watching the rain, muttering not a word.

CHAPTER TWELVE

JAKE BEGAN TO do some figuring. He remembered how the old man made a rough sluice box to work the gravel with. Stroking his beard, Jake tried to place in his mind how it was made. It took flat boards, if his memory served him right, and where would he find flat lumber around here? They could split some of those poles up where they had made the dam. He glanced at Cad and found him sleeping. Pete, with his hat pulled down over his eyes, was also napping.

Well, damn, I can't sit around here all day. The rain was nothing more than a steady drizzle and he'd walked through worse weather than this many a time. Donned in a slicker, hat pulled down low over his eyes, he started off in the direction of the dam. Not to be left, old Blaze trotted up to follow him.

Jake and Blaze walked as far up the stream as they could go before it split. The dam seemed to be holding just fine, and the rain did not seem to be creating a heavy flow of water. Maybe I should go back and roust the two of them out and we could get going. He turned as if to return to camp and then stopped.

No, this was a holiday as well as a panning trip and it was not going to make any difference one way or another, whether they worked today or tomorrow. Besides he wanted to walk further up into the hills anyway.

The left fork of the stream came from high up in the hills above the meadow while the right fork seemed to follow a small canyon. Jake thought he would take the canyon and see where it took him. Blaze was having the time of his life, kicking up his heels and galloping upstream ahead of Jake. Jake was walking with his head down studying the formation of the creek bottom. It all seemed to be pretty much hardpan here. He wished he'd thought to bring his pick. It wasn't that far back to where they had left the tools the day before. He would leave old Blaze to wander up ahead while he slipped back for his pick.

The rain was beginning to fall a little harder now and while he was there, he decided to check on the dam again. It was holding well but the original streambed was gathering water again. *Oh well*, thought Jake, *let her rip, who cares.*

He started back down the canyon to where he had seen the cracks in the bottom of the creek. It was so shallow at that point that the pick could easily penetrate the hardpan without losing sight of the formation. The small crack Jake was working crumbled under the blow of the pick. Laying the tool down, he dug the loose sand and gravel with his forefinger. Gathering a handful he washed it carefully, rolling the sand and gravel between his fingers to be sure it was not gold bearing grit. He worked thus for some time before he came across a sizable nugget. Okay, now, this looked right promising. He worked his way upstream, sifting the gravel as he went. As he rounded a bend in the stream, he could see where the water had worn down the soft center of the stream, leaving shelves exposed high and dry. He was so engrossed in what he was doing, he totally forgot Blaze, and when the agonizing braying scream split the air, he was shaken to his boots. He dropped the pick and stood up listening, again the scream. It was coming from far ahead upstream.

"Blaze, Blaze, old boy, I'm a comin', hold on, son." Jake scrambled over the slippery rocks following the sound of Blaze's cries. He had not realized how high the canyon walls had become as he proceeded upstream. The canyon turned and as Jake rounded the bend, he was stopped short. The whole scene had changed. There were towering cliffs that narrowed in so close they almost seemed to touch. There were many overhanging trees and several arterial waterfalls cascading into the stream. A short distance further upstream was a large waterfall pummeling some hundred feet into the stream. With his heart in his throat he hurried on as best he could. The water began to deepen rapidly as he approached the falls. Certainly Blaze would never go into water that deep. Glancing around, he noticed a narrow ledge to his left and headed for it. Yes, he saw Blaze's wet hoof prints in the sand. How could he travel along that narrow a ledge? *Why*, wondered Jake, *hadn't he returned instead of going deeper into the canyon?*

Jake stumbled along the ledge following Blaze's hoof prints. Then suddenly he heard the mule squeal again. It came from just below the falls. Jake inched along to the base of the falls. The ledge was broken and old Blaze was pawing and struggling to regain his footing. There was a low overhanging tree at that point, and wrapped around the lowest branch was a huge mountain diamondback rattlesnake. He hung precariously with only his tail firmly anchored to the branch. He had evidently struck at the mule which caused the animal to lose his footing and at the same time allowed too much of this heavy body to uncoil from the tree.

Every time the snake would weave back and forth trying to work his body back up into the tree, the mule would resume his struggling. Jake wondered if the snake had indeed bit Blaze and if he could get close enough to loosen the snake from the tree

71

into the gushing waters before he did bite.

Jake pulled his bowie knife out of its sheath and with it in his mouth, inched around a protruding rock. As he did, he came face to face with the rattler on the wide arch of its swing. Without hesitation, he struck out and grabbed the snake right behind the head and with one rapid motion, sliced the rattler in two.

He reached for the terrified Blaze and saw that the mule had slipped into the foaming pool just at the base of that overhanging tree and his hoof was caught in a tangle of roots from which he could not free himself. Jake spoke soothingly. "Whoa, Blaze, old man, easy there fella, it's me, Jake. Hold on, it's not going to do you any good to pull so confounded hard. You'll pull your leg off. Whoa, I say."

The mule was beginning to calm down so Jake reached into the water and tried to pull the roots aside enough to allow Blaze room to free his hoof. The mule pulled but was still caught fast. How the hell did the hoof slip into it in the first place if the roots would not give enough for him to pull out? Jake backed up and took his ten-inch bowie knife once again out of its sheath, then reached down and hacked at the roots until they became more flexible. This time the roots gave and with a mighty heave, Blaze exploded out of the water. He stood shaking and moaning. Jake put his arm around the soaked mule and hugged him, running his hands over Blaze and checking him carefully for signs of snakebite. Finding none, he expelled a sigh of relief.

A chill wind was beginning to rise and darkness had already settled into the canyon by the time Jake and Blaze reached the spot where Jake had dropped his pick. They did not even stop in the darkness to look for it. Jake figured it would be there when he came back.

A voice penetrated the still air. It was Cad. He and Pete were no doubt looking for them.

"Halloooo! Jake! Halloooo!"

"Hallooooo! Cad, here we are."

"Dad blast it all, Jake, where the hell you and that lop-eared mule been anyway?" Cad had made a torch that was having a hard time staying lit with all the rain, and he was a smoking, simmering, ethereal looking figure to Jake, but a welcome sight just the same.

"Come on, Cad, let's find Pete and head for camp. When we get back, I'll tell you all about it."

"What's Blaze limping for? And what's that blood running down his neck?"

"Just wait till we get back to camp. Where's Pete?"

"Pete? Oh, he went up the other fork of the creek. I almost forgot, I was supposed to fire a shot if I found you first." So saying, he raised his pistol and fired. They waited and before long, there was an answering shot.

Pete emerged out of the darkness swearing with relief at the sight of Jake and Blaze. It had been a trying day and they were glad to be heading back to camp. Leaning back against a tree, basking in the warm glow of the fire, with bellies full of rabbit stew, they listened to Jake relate the trials of the day. The rain drizzled forlornly on the tarp cover and it wasn't long before they were all asleep.

CHAPTER THIRTEEN

THE FOLLOWING DAY brought a clear bright sun, as if it had never rained the day before. The trio was ready and raring to go at the stream. This time they took the pans with them. The dam had held and the diverted streambed was about the same as it had been the day before.

They worked diligently shoveling the sand and gravel off the bedrock. Once it had been cleared, they took cooking spoons and carefully cleaned out the sand and gravel from the cracks and potholes. They filled the pans and took them over to the new bed of slow running water, washing, tilting, swirling and dipping, allowing only the heavier dust and small stones to remain. Some gold dust was recovered and nuggets so small they had to be retrieved with tweezers, but nothing of great size. Between the three of them, toiling all day, they only had a scant quarter of a pint jar full by dark.

That evening, after supper chores were completed and all were seated around the campfire, Jake unwrapped a new gold mining pan he had purchased before they left Bodie. He held it up to the firelight and watched the flames cast spears of light to bounce off the gleaming bottom. He ran his hand over its smooth surface. A new pan always thrilled him. It was about 24 inches in diameter and the edges sloped at a 45-degree angle. It made him feel the gold swimming in the bottom. But first he must temper his pan, take off that glorious shine and remove all traces of oil or grease. He rose to his feet and going over to the fire, stoked the glowing embers until they were a nice even bed. He then placed his pan on the bed of coals and sat down to watch. When the pan began to turn red, he quickly fished it out and immersed it into a bucket of cold water. After examining it, he found it needed to be heated once again. He placed it back upon the embers. This time he allowed it to become a little redder before immersing it. As he raised it to the firelight he smiled. *Perfect*, he thought, *a nice even blue color. Ought to be able to see any speck of dust that washes in.* Gently he wiped it dry as if it were a priceless china dish, and placed it in his bag.

The next day they decided to break up the dam and work up in the canyon where Jake found the larger nugget the day of Blaze's mishap. Jake found that the canyon became so narrow that they were getting in each other's way. To work single file made the waters so muddy that the last person in line couldn't see what the gravel and sand in his pan looked like. Pete had an idea.

"I think I'll go back and work up the left fork of the stream. Could be some color up that direction and it has wider banks to work off of."

"Say, that's a great idea, Pete, mind if I join you?" Cad was eagerly questing.

"Suit yerself, Cad, just don't get in my way. You have a knack for creating trouble wherever you go."

"I'll keep out of your way, Pete, it's too confining in this canyon for me."

The two took off together leaving Jake to his own devices. *This is great*, sighed Jake, *now I can work at my own pace*. He took out his new pan, held it up and spit on it for good luck.

Jake worked his way back downstream to where the water had receded and there were several small potholes and cracks in the bedrock. Taking his pick and his crowbar, he chipped carefully away at the cracks. He filled the pan with his pickings and returned to the stream where he allowed the water to flow into the pan. Then swirling the water around and around, returned it with the smaller sand and gravel back to the stream.

By mid-afternoon Jake had almost half a pint jar of fair sized gold nuggets. He wandered back up to the fork of the stream and gazed off in the direction of the left fork.

"Wonder how Pete and Cad are doin' about now," he mused. "Think I'll mosey on up and see for myself."

The stream climbed up slowly, widening as it went. It was shallow and moving a little too rapidly to be a good panning stream. After walking for almost an hour, he came across Pete and Cad. They had found a place where the stream ran through solid rock. The water level had receded enough to expose potholes and crevices and the two men were working feverishly. Jake noticed a pint jar almost full of gold sand and nuggets. *Damn, all the gold in the stream must have fallen here*. He hurried over and began working a spot that appeared to be untouched.

By night they were tired and ready to drop. True bedrock mining was not for the faint of heart. Jake was glad to see Cad was working up a good healthy interest in the job. It was surprising he had that much energy, he was always complaining about how tired he was. Jake had a feeling it was mostly in his mind. All he had ever heard from Cad was how frail and useless he was ever since he was born. Guess it would make a man believe it if he heard it often enough.

They stumbled into camp, made and ate supper in silence,

and piled into their blankets early.

The sun rose in secret the next day. Clouds once again covered the sky and they decided to take the day off from panning and see if they couldn't find where game might possibly be. A small deer would taste good right now. They were getting tired of rabbit. No one wanted to take the time to hunt for anything larger. Their whole efforts were concentrated on panning the stream.

Taking their rifles they headed up the hill back of the camp. At the top of the crest they voted to split up. There was a small grassy spot surrounded by a good brush cover that appealed to Jake. He found a place behind a cluster of rocks and placing his rifle across his lap, settled down to wait.

The morning was cool and fragrant. The dim light of dawn gave a gray and black pencil sketching appearance to the scene below. The straining eye gave life to even the stillest of branches. Jake was beginning to get jumpy. He was just about to rise when a shot rang out, causing him to leap into the air.

A deep southern voice vented the air with, "Yahoo, I got him."

"Yeah, and you damn near got me in the bargain," Jake complained. "Damn, he was practically down the back of my neck!" Not 50 feet from where Jake had been sitting lay a deer. Jake swung his head around as a crashing occurred across the field and Pete came bounding out from behind the far bushes holding his rifle in the air.

"How about that, Jake, downed him with one shot," Pete shouted gleefully.

"He's a beaut, all right, what do ya say we dress him and string him up in yonder trees over there?"

"Fine with me," said Pete as he reached for his hunting knife. It was a nice two-point buck weighing probably around 100 pounds.

"Boy, is he going to taste good tonight," drooled Pete. "I can hardly wait." As they busied themselves dressing the buck, they heard a shot, then another, then another.

"Now what the hell is he shooting at?" said Pete. "Whatever it is should be damn sure dead or halfway into the next county by now."

Jake chuckled, Pete was always at poor Cad's throat. It seemed that if Cad was going to do or say anything stupid, it was within eyeshot or earshot of Pete. The shots were at some distance and sounded as if they came from over in the direction of camp.

Both Jake and Pete stopped what they were doing and stared at each other. Camp! They dropped the deer and struck off at a run up the hill. At the top they were almost knocked down by a covey of quail as they flew low over the summit. Quail? Was that what Cad was shooting at? Not someone trying to take over the camp? They stood and listened. Not another sound. Then they saw Cad emerge out of the trees and pick up three quail, one for each shot. The two men slumped, hung their limp arms to their sides and sighed in relief. Well, with Cad, one couldn't be too careful. It could just as easy been the other way around. They turned and headed back for the deer.

When they came to where they had left the deer, they found a bloody trail where the deer had been dragged off down the hill.

"Wal, I'll be a dirty son-of-a-bitch!" bellered Pete. Grabbing his rifle, he started off following the trail. "I ain't goin' ta let some other varmint make off with my catch, no, sir, I jest ain't agoin' ta let that happen."

Jake stood there laughing softly. He couldn't help it. Poor Cad strikes again. No matter what, Cad always managed to get to Pete. Shouldering his rifle, he strode off after Pete. Blam! Blam! Jake stopped short, whipping his rifle into position.

"Gawd damn thief," he could hear Pete swear. "I'll blow yer thieven guts out." Blam!

Jake took off at a trot and came upon Pete, rifle still smoking, and looked in the direction of the trembling barrel. There on the ground lay a large black bear. The deer had been mauled beyond their consumption, but now they had bear meat instead of venison. *Oh, well, all's well that ends well*, thought Jake.

They began trying to pull the bear around to dress him. "You know, Pete, we're going to have to get some rope and one of the mules to haul this beast back to camp. He must weigh three hundred pounds."

"Yeah, he ain't no light weight. You all stay here and I'll go fetch some rope and old Blaze. I'll be right back."

A crash of brush and a rusty bray told Jake of Pete's return. "Hey, Jake, guess what? When I got back to camp I found Cad fixin' those quail fer lunch. Damn, but that makes my mouth water."

He dismounted and threw the end of the rope to Jake. They tied the rope around the bear's four legs, then threw the other end over a low hanging branch, securing it to the horn on Blaze's pack harness. Jake took Blaze by the halter and ordered him to back. Well, that was all fine and dandy but when that bear began to rise off the ground, old Blaze took one look at that shaggy beast, let out a string of squeaking brays, and started to buck and pull in an attempt to escape. This made the bear rise and fall in a grotesque manner, making it even more threatening to the already frightened mule.

Jake was sent sprawling downhill while Pete was still hanging on to the end of the rope, being drawn up and down with each rise and fall of the bear. Blaze was not to be consoled. A bear was not to be fooled with in his book of rules, and this one was acting mighty spooky.

Jake got up and ran back to the bucking Blaze. He grabbed the halter and gave it a mighty yank, throwing the mule off balance and crashing to its knees. "Whoa, damn you, Blaze, what the hell is the matter with you anyway?" As Blaze fell to his knees, he brought the dangling Pete crashing up into the branch where it almost knocked him senseless. He let go of the rope and sat nursing his head in his hands.

"Ooooh, my head. Where did you find that stupid, hair-brained red son-of-a-bitch when you bought him? In the loony bin?"

Jake was too busy trying to settle the fuming Blaze to answer Pete.

They spent the next hour trying to introduce Blaze to the dead bear. It was a comedy of errors. He was the biggest damn mule this side of Missouri and he was not going to let anyone talk him into hauling any old bear.

Exhausted, they sat on the ground resting and mumbling about the world's stupidest mule. "Aaah! Why didn't I think of it before!" He stood up, unhitched the mule from the bear and led him a short distance off. Then, taking off his bandana, he tied it around the mule's eyes and led him back to the rope, tying it to the pack harness. He then led Blaze back up the hill. It worked. Pete ran under the branch, throwing his end over as he ran, and secured it in place. Jake backed Blaze down under the bear, then grabbing the other end with Pete, they eased the bear down onto Blaze's back. The mule groaned under the weight but held fast. They then led the mule blindfolded back into camp.

As they approached, the delightful aroma of roasting quail struck their nostrils. Ah! What a feast awaited them.

They pulled up under a tree where they once again threw the rope over the branch and the three of them hauled the bear up off of Blaze's back. Jake led him still blindfolded, off into the meadow before unhitching the pack harness and removing the blindfold. The mule moaned and rubbed his head up and down on Jake's chest.

"Get outta here, you dad blasted dummy. You almost cost us

our bear. Sometimes you are the biggest ass I know. Other times, you almost think like a human. Now, get." He slapped the mule on the rump and headed back to camp.

They ate Cad's quail with great gusto. "Man, Cad, this is just about the greatest food I've tasted since I left Texas," Pete said, the juice running down his chin.

"Thanks, Pete. When I saw that covey of quail, I thought they would make us a good lunch, and decided to leave the deer to you fellows."

After lunch, they set Cad to digging a roasting pit while Jake and Pete skinned the bear. There must have been two hundred pounds of dressed meat in that bear. Pete carved out a huge roast and set it aside. Then he carved out several more roasts and a whole raft of steaks.

Cad went off down to the creek where they had small nail kegs soaking in the water to swell and brought them back. The steaks were salted heavily, packed in the barrels, placed in canvas bags and buried in the ground to help preserve them.

The rest of the meat was stripped, salted and laid out to dry. Cad had been busy making drying racks while Jake and Pete were dressing the bear. Once the meat was stripped, Pete scraped at the lining of the hide to remove the membrane. It was a nice large hide. Pete looked at Jake. "My boy, Jed, would like this for his bed. Do either of you mind if I keep it?"

"Lord, no, Pete, every boy should have a token treasure like that." Cad smiled. "What do you say, Jake?"

"As far as I'm concerned, it's his. All you have to do is talk this silly ass into carrying it back for you."

"Maybe I can talk Mabel into carrying it for me. She's a nice, quiet mule, not like that opinioned jug-headed, locomotive sized hunk of trouble you have." Cad slapped his knee and laughed loudly. Jake was not much amused at Pete's description of his beloved Blaze.

Jake took the roast, skewered it on a long pole, then it was hung in the roasting pit. A large fire had been made and when the coals were roaring hot, a layer of stones were placed on top of them. Another fire had been built on top of the stones and when it had turned to coals, the meat was lowered into the pit for roasting. Soon the air was filled with the smell of simmering juices as they dripped on the heated stones.

Jake continued salting strips of meat Pete was carving and placing them on the racks to dry. It was an all day job and they were not quite finished by the time the roast was. Cad had stopped making racks and had placed potatoes in a pan and put the pan over the coals to cook. He then made a Dutch oven full of biscuits.

Jake and Pete placed the rest of the meat in a burlap bag and raised it high into the pine tree until they could get around to it the next day.

As the men prepared to down the feast, Jake produced two brown jugs of Bodie's finest whiskey.

The meal turned in a rollicking good time and before the moon had risen, the three men were dead drunk. They laughed and sang and pranced around the meadow like buffoons. Suddenly, Cad stopped and said, "Hey, anyone for a moonlight dip?"

"Hell, yes," answered the other two. With that they stripped down to the bare essentials and plunged into the deepest part of the meadow pool.

All of the commotion and the smell of fresh meat attracted the attention of the neighborhood cougar. Now this young male cougar was under the impression this was his territory so he wandered down from his lair in the high rocks to see if he could get himself invited to the party. It seemed that the humans were enjoying themselves down in the pool and seeing no reason to interrupt their fun, the big cat padded his way to where the burlap sack was hanging in the tree just awaiting his pleasure. The only problem was that it was too high. He settled back on his haunches and leapt into the air, wrapping his front legs around the burlap bag.

In the meantime, Jake, Cad and Pete were through with their icy-cold dip and were headed, bare-assed, back across the meadow to the warmth of the fire pit. By the time they reached the fire, they could see the big cat dangling in the air.

"Gawd damn," croaked Pete, "look what's hangin' up thar above our haids, whar's my rifle, whar's my gun, whar the hell's my clothes?" He was running around in circles. Jake and Cad stood there with their mouths open, shivering and staring up into the tree. They couldn't make up their minds who looked the funniest, the cat hanging there snarling and running the air with his hind feet, or Pete, naked, running around looking for his clothes or his gun, whichever came first.

The cat, in trying to climb up the rope and into the tree, got the bag to swinging, his sharp claws ripped at the rope until it gave way, and on the farthest out swing, the bag, cat and all fell tail first into the smoldering fire pit. With a scream and a fantastic leap, the cougar cleared the pit, the second leap took him over the heads of our naked trio and out into the forest behind the camp.

"Jesus," said Cad, "did you see that? I'll bet he has four of the sorest burned feet in the mountains."

"Here," said Jake, "help me get this bag out of the pit before it catches fire." Together they pulled the smoldering burlap out and back up into the tree.

They finally found their clothes, which were still out in the meadow, and by the time they were dressed, were once again sober. It had been a fun night and they would spend many a night to come, reminiscing around the campfires of the future.

CHAPTER FOURTEEN

THE BEAR MEAT salted and set out on racks to dry over the smoking fire pit was finished before noon. The three men ate a silent meal and sat looking at each other.

"Wal," drawled Pete, "what do we do now?"

"We still have all of our panning equipment up creek, does anyone want to take up the gold fight?" Jake asked.

Pete sat back and rolled a cigarette, whipped a match against his jeans leg and lit it. Through the cloud of smoke, he said, "I think we should gather the rest of our meat and head for home. My family will be good and sore at me now for being away so long."

Jake looked long at Cad. "Was wonderin', Cad, do you suppose you could stay out of trouble now when we go back to Bodie?"

"Well, Jake, I guess you could say that four weeks in the mountains have cleared my head some."

"Cleared yer haid up? Hell, Cad, ya ain't got no haid," bantered Pete. The three men laughed and set about making preparations for the next day's hunt.

Early the following morning, Jake and Pete headed for the small clearing on the far side of the hill. Cad decided to stay behind and pack up the mining tools that were left scattered up and down the banks of the stream. He also set more barrels into the meadow pool to soak. The drying racks were full so he made up a few new ones. By the time he finished his chores, he heard Jake and Pete coming down the hill.

"Halloo, Cad, put on the coffee pot and start breakfast, the mighty hunters have returned and we're starving."

Cad chuckled and started the preparations for breakfast. He dumped the coffee pot into the water barrel, threw some coffee grounds in and set it on the grate over the fire pit. Humming to himself, he placed a glob of bacon grease in the pan and broke in half a dozen eggs. It was a good thing they were getting ready to leave, the eggs were getting a mite old and he was afraid he would have to throw out the rest as it was. They would just have to live off their meat until time to leave.

Cad glanced up from his meal-making as the other two approached. "What in the hell? Hey, where the hell's the deer?"

"Wal, I think someone must've tipped them off. We sat up there until our butts got numb and nothin' even moved. And besides, our bellies began growling so loud, it chased everything else away."

Jake leaned his rifle against the tree, rubbed his bottom saying, "We're going out again this evening, if you want to go along, Cad."

"No, I think I'll just stay around camp. I'm not much of a hunter and I'm sure, with my luck. I'd just be in the way."

The three men ate their breakfast, leaned back against the tree, Pete rolled a cigarette, and they talked small talk the rest of the morning.

The subject of Bodie and the trouble brewing there never came up in the conversation. It all seemed a yesteryear away.

Cad's idea of smoking the rest of the meat seemed like a good idea and they helped him make new racks, hanging them over the fire pit high enough so as not to catch fire.

It was late afternoon so the men decided to eat an early supper before heading up over the hill again. As they were sitting there silently eating, Jake looked up across the meadow and dropped his mouth.

"Well, I'll be God damn, look over there, fellas, and tell me if I'm seeing things."

They looked up slowly and there at the far end of the meadow was a buck and two doe grazing peacefully. Jake slowly and carefully reached for his rifle, sighting over the barrel he aimed deliberately for the buck. Blam! Great shot, right through the head. The buck took two fantastic bounds and keeled over dead. Picking up their knives, they headed off down the meadow to the dead buck. He was a nice two pointer and they figured he would dress out at about sixty pounds of fresh meat. It was almost dark by the time they were ready to strip the meat for smoking. They could keep the fire going all night, dowsing it now and again to keep it smoking. The rest they would put in the barrels Cad had been soaking.

They worked quickly, making jokes and enjoying the cool evening breezes.

"We better get all this meat worked up and over the smoker or we'll attract our friend the cougar again," Cad said.

It was well on to midnight when all was completed and the mess cleaned up and burned.

The following days were spent rounding up all the gear and packing up the meat and remaining supplies. As the day approached for their departure, the weather changed. Clouds rolled in and it looked as if it would be foggy and musty for their trip home.

The mules were all loaded and the lean-to scattered and they were on their way by noon.

At the bottom of the hill Jake stopped and turned to have a last look at what had been their home for over a month. "Hey, wait," Jake called, "what does this look like, fellas? It looks like more than fog to me." He raised his nose and smelled the air. Nothing, well maybe he was making more of it than it really was.

"I don't see nothin'," Pete said.

"Me neither," sighed Cad. "Jake is such a worry wart."

They turned and made their way down the mountain toward home.

CHAPTER FIFTEEN

SMOKE ROLLED ACROSS the bottom of the mountains like wayward clouds. Blaze set his feet and brayed. Jake dismounted and pulled at the reins but the big mule just rolled his eyes in fear as smoke cut off his vision. "Gol dang it, Blaze, you are the most stubborn animal I ever saw. Can't ya take life in stride once in awhile?" Blaze swung around and headed back up the mountain dragging Jake behind him.

Pete slapped his leg and guffawed. "Jake, ya got the most headstrong stubborn mule in all California. How the hell ya gonna get him off the mountain?"

Jake bolted behind a tree and wrapped the reins around the trunk. Blaze pulled and stomped until Jake was afraid he would break the reins. Working one handed, first one hand then the other, he stripped off his jacket and tied it around the stupid mule's head. Blaze immediately came to a stand still, standing there trembling behind the tree trunk. Jake unwound the reins and walked the subdued mule back to where Pete and Cad were waiting. The smoke was wafting by in ever thickening streams the closer they got to the bottom.

"I wonder where the fire is?" Jake said. "It seems like we're heading right into it."

Pete stood up in the saddle and reached for a branch in the pine tree, climbing as high as he could safely go. Taking the tattered binoculars from around his neck, he scanned the area. "Holy sagebrush, Gawd damn, we're surrounded by fire. The trail we came up from Bodie is in flames and I can't see nothin' up Carson City way."

"Look back up toward the meadow and tell me what you see," Jake asked.

"All I can see is some smoke. Cain't tell if the fire is up that high."

"Maybe that damn mule is smarter than we are. He was headed back up the mountain."

Pete climbed back down out of the tree. "Wal, what air we gonna do?"

Jake looked at him open mouthed. "I don't know, can't you think of something?"

"Guess we outta follow Blaze's idea and head back up," Pete whispered.

"What ya whisperin' for, Pete, are ya afraid I might hear ya?" Cad chuckled.

"No, I'm afraid Blaze might hear me and get the big head. Hell, Cad, I don't know why I was whisperin'."

Cad laughed while Pete glowered at him. Jake took the jacket off Blaze's head, climbed into the saddle and gave the mule his head. They all followed him back up to the meadow. The air was clear and cool without a hint of smoke. They dismounted and looked inquiringly at Jake.

"Why is everyone looking at me? The only thing I know is there is fire down there and none up here. If we go straight ahead we'll be at the top of Buckey Mountain where we hunted the first day, and if we turn right at the top we can go to Iceberg

Meadows and cut northeast toward Walker Lake. I don't know where the fire started but at the bottom of the mountains from up there, is the trail to Bodie from Carson City. I'm sure we can get home from there."

They stared at Jake a few minutes before Pete said, "Hell, Jake, how do you know we can make it? Have you ever been up to Iceberg Meadows?"

"No, I have not been there but I have a map that was given to me by an old miner. He was all over these hills before ending up in Idaho. That's where I met him. He was the one that told me about the sluice box. And that's how I knew about these little meadows where we stayed."

As Jake talked, a billow of smoke blew up from below upsetting Blaze once again. "I'm just going to have to blindfold you until we get home if you don't stop acting like a jackass," Jake said as he steadied the big mule.

"Yeah, well, jackass is what he is, ain't it?" Pete drawled. It was clear he had no liking for the mule.

"I know you don't like him, Pete, but he is smart. He knew where there was no fire, now it looks like the wind has shifted and it's headed this way. Let's quit arguing and get going."

Jake attempted to mount Blaze but the mule was not having any, thank you. "God damn it, Blaze, behave yourself." Jake pulled the reins around until the mule was almost toppling over, then quickly mounted while Blaze regained his footing. "Now, let's get going, otherwise we'll be in for trouble."

Jake moved out and around the small pool where they had taken their midnight dip and headed up Buckley Peak. He could see the fire beginning to work its way up the south side of the mountain. They headed north. Blaze rolled his eyes and frothed at the mouth all the way. Along toward evening, they descended into Iceberg Meadows. They stopped just long enough to water the mules and break out one of the dried meat packs. Jake opened one of his saddlebags and took out his crude map. They sat down and laid it out between them.

"Here's where I figure we can cut back to Bodie if the fire hasn't reached that far. Otherwise, we will have to go farther north, cut east and come out around Walker Lake. Then we can head south for Bodie. I sure as hell hope the fire hasn't gotten into town."

After a brief rest, they mounted up and headed north again. The air was still clear and that raised the men's hopes. The hills became lower and before they knew it, they were out on the desert floor. The fire seemed to be everywhere. All the animals became so nervous they had to head back up into the hills. The darkness of night gave them a full view of where the flames were concentrated. The line of fire seemed to spread from California to the far reaches of Nevada. Now it seemed hopeless.

"Damn," exclaimed Pete as he stood beside Jake, "what now?"

"I don't know, Pete, but I think we had better proceed on foot for a spell. I'm sure I'm going to have to lead Blaze blindfolded if we go through fire. If we go any further north we'll end up on the trail to Carson City. I suggest we rough camp here tonight and see what develops in the morning. For that matter, we could take turns keeping watch on that line of fire during the night. If it starts to move up this mountain, we'll move on out ahead of it. We won't unpack the mules, it'd take too much time if we have to move out in a hurry."

Cad took out a pack of the dried meat and passed it around saying, "I'll take the first watch. I don't suppose we want to start a fire to make coffee? Right?"

"I guess not," chuckled Pete, "it'd probably start that ten ton jackass of Jake's to buckin' and jumpin' and throwin' our gear all over Iceberg Meadows." Cad threw back his head and laughed loudly. Jake was not impressed with the jibe.

Sometime in the early morning hours on Pete's watch, the

wind changed and backtracked the smoke and line of fire. Pete shook Jake, kicked Cad and grabbed for his mule yelling, "Look lively thar, fellas, the fire is backtracking and if we move smartly we could strike a trail right ahead of where the fire ended. Might be able to head directly into Bodie from there."

Pete climbed into the saddle and headed down the hill followed by Jake and Cad. The mules were too heavily loaded to break into a run and took off at a gut wrenching hard trot. Pots and pans jangled and bumped as they wove their way around spots of still burning brush. Amazing enough, old Blaze didn't put up a fuss and they made good time for the first couple of hours.

As they moved further east, they noticed that smoke merged with the trail up ahead which caused them to move a little more northeast. They kept easing that direction until they were heading due north again.

Jake stopped and turned in the saddle to confront the other two. It was blistering hot, desert heat made hotter by winds heated to furnace temperatures. He took off his hat, wiping the sweat from his brow and the inside of the brim. The mules were dripping wet and there was not a tree or bush to help them escape the sun.

"I don't think this is leading us anywhere. We seem to be going farther and farther away from Bodie. It looks like the whole damn desert is in flames. And it's so damn hot, mule turds are burning up before they even hit the ground. I see a small ridge over there a ways. Let's go over there and get up a little higher. Perhaps we can see just where this hell fire is going."

Jake dismounted and taking one of his canteens, poured a small amount into his hand and rubbed it into Blaze's mouth, then took a long drink for himself. The others did likewise. Jake also gave the little pack mule a mouthful hoping they would come to more water before the canteens went dry.

By the time they reached the ridge the sun was beginning to drop down behind the western Sierras. That would soon give them a reprieve from the steel hot sun. Dismounting, they shaded their eyes and stared in the direction of Bodie. The fire spread a long line between them and the town. There was no way of telling if it had reached the town itself. It looked like the only way was to head to Walker Lake and down and over to Mono Lake, then up to Bodie. They stood there wilting and waiting for sunset.

"I'm getting so damn hungry I could eat one of these mules. I don't want any more of the salted meat. It only makes me thirsty and we don't have any fruit or vegetables left. So, Jake, what do you think we should do?" Cad squatted in the shadow of his mule and squinted at Jake.

"Why is it all of the decisions are up to me? Every time we have to decide something, it's Jake this and Jake that. Jesus, Pete, you've lived in this desert longer than I have, you've always had good ideas, let's hear from you."

"Yeah, I've lived here longer than you but I never leave camp to go any farther than to Bodie. You have been all over this country."

"Okay, then, I say this. We rest awhile, take a good long drink, head out for Walker Lake, water the mules and head for Mono Lake. From there we can go up into the hills and home." Jake stood up, slapped his hat on his leg, spat on the ground and turned his back on the rest.

Jake lay back against a little pile of sage branches, pulled his hat over his eyes and drifted off to sleep.

The trail to Mono Lake was clear of fire and they made good time. By evening they could see smoke beginning to blow in their direction. They rested for a few hours, catching what sleep they could. A blinding light and crash of thunder startled everyone to their feet. Another flash and a torrent of fresh cool rain spread across the desert putting out the areas of fires still burning. The trio jumped up and down, rubbing their faces in the welcome rain, laughing and scaring the mules. They gathered their wits and hit the trail up into the hills and home.

CHAPTER SIXTEEN

IT WAS SOME time now since the mountain trip and Cad seemed to have mellowed out, at least for the time being. He was content to stay around the area, even though he was less inclined to work in the mine. This bothered Jake some. Where did all that enthusiasm go he exhibited in the mountains? He supposed he should be thankful Cad kept himself out of trouble.

These last few weeks Jake had worked the mine he called his Full House, until the pile of rubble outside the hut was becoming a veritable mountain. Somehow this visible evidence was going to have to be removed. *That would be a good job for Cad*, Jake thought. *He can bring down the mules and haul this mess off somewhere and dump it.*

Cad was agreeable and swung the shovel energetically, filling several sacks with rocks and dirt. He whistled and sang as he worked, bringing the mules down where he threw the sacks over their backs and trotted away. He dumped them in the area of the first mine giving the impression there was still activity there. The only sour note on an otherwise favorable deed came out of Cad's mouth. "Lordy, Lordy!" Jake slapped as he hollered out loud, "I hope that fool does not attract everyone in the state of California with his serenading. He has no realization of the danger he puts us all in. Sometimes I feel like he hasn't a speck of reasoning power in his head, but Cad has always been that way."

The mine was yielding a goodly amount of gold bearing quartz now and not so much plain rock. Jake eyed his supply of quartz on hand and a cold feeling crept up his spine. If someone should bust in right now, they could see what a haul he was getting out of his own house. "I might just end up with another bullet that 'found something important' to hit this time," Jake muttered.

Jake walked back and forth, stroking his beard and thinking of what to do. He could not use the false teeth trick again, too many people in Carson City saw that one, especially that Lord fellow. He was going to have to think of something else. Maybe Cad would have a good idea. Just at that moment Cad came back down the hill from his last trip.

He's been gone a long time, wonder where he's been, Jake thought hesitantly.

Cad came bursting through the door. "Hey, guess what I found? An old, old abandoned mine, it must have been a whopper in its time. I thought this was supposed to be a relatively new area for gold. Well, someone else was working this territory long before we ever got here. Come on out and take a look."

Jake and Cad rode off in the direction of Jake's first claim, then Cad led him over the hill and down the other side. They traveled for some distance until they came to an almost overgrown old wagon trail. They turned and rode down the trail for almost a quarter of a mile. On the left side of the trail was a dry creek bed heavily studded on both sides with scrub willows. Here Cad stopped and dismounted. Parting the willows, they saw the partially caved in opening to a mine. Scrambling over large boulders and fallen beams, they found themselves inside a large cavern.

Jake held up his hand saying, "Hold it a minute, Cad, let me strike a match so I can see where the hell we are."

He reached into his pocket and took out a match, heisted his leg and struck it on the seat of his pants. As the match flared they gasped, "Ahhhhh! Did you see that? Go back and get a stick or something that will burn a little longer."

They stumbled over each other on the way out. "Quick, grab that dead bush over there, no, no, that one. Yeah, that's it. Here, let's get back in there a ways before we light it." They were so excited they could hardly get the bush lighted and when they did, the sight that confronted them made their mouths gape open. There before them yawned a huge black hole. Lying down on their bellies, they inched their way over to the edge. Peering over and holding the burning bush out over the hole, they strained to see if they could find a bottom. None. Just below the edge at about arm's length ran a shelf almost all the way around. The rest was just a bottomless pit. It was evident that this was no mine but a large underground cavern.

Jake nudged Cad. "Let's back up outta here before our fire goes completely out."

Outside again, the two men looked at each other. "Let's keep this to ourselves, Cad, okay? It might come in handy sometime."

They did what they could to hide the entrance to the cave, mounted the mules and rode on down the trail. Jake wanted to find out just where the trail went. It seemed to wind around and head for Mono Lake. Then it turned and emerged on the main road heading once again for Bodie. They followed it back to the hut, unsaddled the mules in the late twilight, and gathered wood for the evening meal.

Jake and Cad made preparations for the supper in silence.

"What's on your mind, Jake? You're awfully quiet."

"Yeah? Well, I'm thinking. You know, I've got to do something about this ore that's building up. Finding that cave is giving me an idea. Just let me mull it over a bit more, then we'll talk about it."

They finished their supper which consisted of some of the dried bear meat from their trip, and as they sat by the fire with coffee cups in hand, Jake began to talk.

"Cad, you know, if I make some kind of move that looks like I'm packing gold ore out of here, I'm not going to make it to the bottom of the grade before someone tries to take a shot at me. I don't have the proper material to extract the gold from the quartz and I don't want to go buying the stuff in Bodie for that would just draw attention to me. So, I've got to devise a plan to haul it out by wagon. I can borrow Pete's old wagon, I'm sure, and I can hide the sacks of gold ore on that shelf you found in the cave. But how can I arrange to get it there without being spotted? I don't want anyone to know I'm gone."

"Let's see, Jake, you don't want anyone to see you leave, so you need some kind of diversion. Something that will make everyone in Bodie think you're still around. How about me? You know the ladies have been after me to give a concert. I could go talk to them. You know, plan some big bang up concert that would be of interest to everyone. Something like one night for one kind of music and one night for another, that would give you two nights to plan your departure. What do you think?"

"Hmmmm!" mused Jake. "That may be just what I need." Jake stood and began pacing the floor. He could use those two days to pack the gold ore over to the cave and place it on the shelf. He'd better go talk to Pete and see if the wagon would be available on the weeks he would need it.

Cad did his part booking two days, Tuesday and Thursday

of next week. Pete said he wasn't going to need the old wagon for some time. He had picked up a smaller buggy to pack supplies in and probably would never need the big one again.

"Maybe I could buy the old one from you? Name me a price."

"Naw, you can have the blamed thing. Then if I need it fer somethin' I can borrow it back."

Jake and Pete stood, hands on hips and looked silently at the wagon. Jake stooped over and examined the underneath of the wagon. "Say, Pete, what's this double bed all about?"

"Wal, I put that in fer our trip across Texas. That ole' rattletrap was pretty old at that time and I didn't want all our household goods and kids scattered across the desert. Everyone here knows about it. I've lent it out a few times fer heavy duty haulin'. Some of the boards are busted but you could replace them. What ya got in mind, Jake?"

Jake squinted at Pete and spoke in tones barely above a whisper. He told him of the cave Cad found and the supply of gold quartz gathering in the hut. Also of Cad's concerts coming up next week so he could pack the ore to the cave for safekeeping.

On the night of the first concert, Jake hurriedly packed the mules and headed for the caves. He had taken a lantern along to light his way into the cave without falling into that awful gaping hole. He placed the bags of ore on the ledge and led the mules back to the hut. He had just finished putting the mules away when Cad came home. He was elated with the way the concert had gone and expounded elaborately. It was plain to Jake that the singing was far more exhilarating to him than digging for gold.

On Thursday Jake made his second pilgrimage to the cave, getting home later than before, to find Cad already home and asleep. Jake wrinkled his nose as he entered the hut and shook his head. The smell of liquor was heavy in the air. Damn, he hoped Cad had not been loose lipped to some dance hall gal. It would be terrible to lose all the ore now. *Oh boy*, Jake sighed heavily, blew out the lantern and retired for the night.

CHAPTER SEVENTEEN

THE FOLLOWING DAY Cad arose and, with Jake, began to make plans for Cad's day in Bodie. What to say, what to do and above all, what *not* to say and who not to say it to. "And, God damn it, Cad, please CONTROL YOUR DRINKING."

The sun blazed hot early on the morning of the proposed trip and made any activity strenuous. Cad complained bitterly all the way to Pete's about the weather in that Godforsaken country.

They pulled the wagon around and hitched all four mules to it. Jake said his farewells with only head nods and headed off down the road to Mono Lake. He was so pleased with himself that the plan was working so well that he became overconfident.

About a mile down the road two men confronted him. He instantly recognized them as the two men he had seen in Carson City at the Wells Fargo office, talking to Mr. Lord. A wave of fear touched him lightly and he made a move to place himself in a more convenient position to his gun. As he did so he heard several horses behind him. He looked back over his shoulder and saw the men he had always figured were the ones who shot him at the mine. It was obvious to Jake that they were all one gang. It wouldn't surprise me any if this bunch was the infamous Mr. Lord's outlaw gang everyone was suspicious of in Carson City.

"Wal, now, lookie here, pard. Here's our little shriveled up friend. Now how the hell do ya suppose he managed to survive all those bullets?" This came from behind him but he never let his eyes leave the two men in front of him.

One of them rode down and took the lead mule's rein, leering evilly at Jake. The other, holding his rifle across the front of his saddle, smiled and replied, "Don't know, Cappy, but I reckon he must've found more gold or he wouldn't still be in these parts. Whatcha got in the wagon, runt?"

"Nothing," Jake responded.

"Wal, now, whar ya goin' then, runt?"

"Ain't goin' nowhere," said Jake, "need wood and now's the only time I could borrow a wagon."

"Wood," snorted Cappy, "now that's a likely story. Ain't wood gatherin' time yet, gotta be another reason. You got four mules hitched, wood ain't that heavy, now is it?"

"Can't see workin' two mules to death when I got four to do the job. What's so damn funny about a man going for wood anyway?"

"Nothin', except it's in the middle of August and so Gawd damn hot ya could fry eggs on the sand."

Out of the corner of his eye he could see two more men approaching.

"Told ya, damn it, I gotta go when I can borrow the wagon. And besides, I gotta have wood to cook with so I figured I might just as well load up. Now, if you would just get outta my way, I'll go on down to the mill."

"Wal, it seems like yer carryin' a lotta stuff in that wagon for just a jaunt to the mill."

"Can't help what I'm carryin'. I'm not strong and it takes me a long time to load a wagon so it takes me two days. You bastards got all the gold I had, including the mine. What the hell do ya want with me now?"

"Just figure yer lyin', that's all. Think me and the boys will go with ya. Seen' as how ya got that wagon, we'll take a load ourselves."

With that, they turned loose the reins, gave the mules a slap, and surrounding the wagon, followed Jake down the road. Inside Jake was boiling.

The son-of-a-bitches! Now what in the hell were they up to? One of the men jumped aboard the wagon and began going through Jake's things. Of course they could find nothing because at this point there was nothing to find. Then he began going over the wagon looking for false bottoms or extra panels and not finding any, got back on his horse. *Maybe he'll leave now*, thought Jake, but no, they followed along. By early afternoon they arrived at the mill where everyone swung into action and helped load the wagon. Jake pulled out a pouch filled with a small amount of gold dust. He was thankful he had brought it along and paid the man for his wood.

"Wait a minute," the mill man said, "this ain't enough."

Jake turned and looked at the man they called Cappy and said, "I thought you were going to buy one of these loads. Where's your money?"

"Haw! Haw! Now what made you think we were goin' ta pay fer our load of wood? Just fetch up the money, runt."

Looking at the mill man, he asked him to help pull off enough wood so that what gold he had would pay for it. The mill man sized up the rough looking men that came with Jake and figured he knew what was happening. "I'll tell you what, friend, we'll call it square this time but on your next run you can drop it off or have a friend do it for you."

"That's right neighborly of ya. I'll just take ya up on it."

Jake turned the wagon around and headed back to Bodie. *Hell and damnation, what am I going to do now?* Cappy's voice broke into his thoughts. "Seems ta me a feller goin' fer wood would be sure ta take along enough gold ta pay fer it, wouldn't ya say so, boys?"

"Yeah, Cap, what do ya think he was really goin' fer?"

"Wood, damn ya, wood. I would have had enough gold if you bastards had coughed up the money for your own wood. I ain't got much gold, you bastards got all I had. I can't even scratch enough together to get the hell outta this damn town."

It was obvious the men did not believe him. The harder he tried to convince them, the less they believed him. Jake realized that for the first time in his life, he had lost the calm wit by which he lived. A man with no physical strength had to learn to live by his wits if he wished to survive. And here he was, totally defenseless. His gun lay useless beneath the seat of the wagon and he was quite obviously nervous. The sweat was rolling off him in streams. The day was boiling hot and the mules were tired and dragging. One of the men began beating the lead mule who promptly sat down.

"Here now, Gawd damn you, leave those mules alone. You could beat old Blaze to death and he'll never move. You have to talk gently to him. Make him understand what you want him to do and why. You just get yourself outta the way."

With that the man twirled around in the saddle and struck Jake with his rope full across the face. "You'd better get that jackass movin' or I'll beat the hide off that ugly body of yours."

"Neil, Gawd damn it, what the hell are ya tryin' to do?" Cappy yelled. "We'll never get up this hill if ya don't simmer down. All right, all of ya, get down and let's rest. The horses are all wet and, and by Gawd, so am I. And if'n ya don't relax, we'll be a'shootin' each other."

The late afternoon sun was like a furnace and the trip home

was uphill and tiring. Jake walked up to Blaze who still sat in the middle of the road whimpering. If the situation wasn't so serious, he could have seen the humor in the incident. He grabbed the mule by the ears and drew his head down to his chest where he began stroking his muzzle and talking to him. The mule heaved a sigh, closed his eyes and allowed himself to be sweet-talked out of his stubbornness, but he still sat sulking and Jake dropped down in the dust in the shade of the mule to rest.

He closed his eyes and thought. Somehow he was going to have to convince these men that they were wasting their time. He realized the loss of his composure led them to believe he was lying and all the frustrating little things kept happening to add to his nervousness. This day had been wasted and now he needed to construct a new plan for another day.

Time was running out. He was startled out of his reverie by Cappy yelling, "Now get that Gawd damn mule to his feet or we won't get back to Bodie till mawnin'."

Jake stood up and as he did so, Blaze got to his feet. They all moved forward slowly. Tempers were short and Jake feared they might do their worst before they got back.

Jake figured it was about two in the morning when they pulled into Bodie. Everyone was bone tired and the wagon was left loaded until next morning. They tied Jake's hands behind his back and forced him to spend the night down in the road. There was no wagon trail up to the hut so they spent the night where they were. The mules were not allowed to have their harnesses removed and sagged forlornly in them. The only one who complained was Blaze who sat down and began to moan, which he kept up most of the night. By dawn, all were back on their feet. Cappy reached down and picked Jake up by his shirt and said, "Now you unhitch them mules and turn them loose. And if I hear one more moan outta that lop-eared-son-of-a-bitch, I'm gonna blow his head off."

Jake hurried to comply with his commands. He wished that damn mule wasn't such a spoiled baby but he loved that animal and Blaze loved him. While Jake unhitched the mules, Blaze licked the salt off Jake's face and neck. "Stop that, Gawd damn it, you've got us in enough trouble, now take the rest and get!"

The mules wandered on up the trail to the hut. Jake wondered where Cad was. There should have been smoke by now. He was somewhat worried, maybe they had found Cad and killed him, or forced him to talk. As they all walked up to the hut, Cappy pointed a gun at Jake's head and said, "Now you tell me where the gold is."

"I ain't got no gold," argued Jake. "Go take a look in the shack, two more small bags just like the one I had at the mill, that's all."

Jake had hung an Indian blanket over the entrance to his mine before he left and cleaned the rubble out the room. He knew they would not see anything if they did go in.

"Hell, man, you mean you were tellin' the truth all along? I've got a good mind to…"

"Hey, Cappy, someone's comin'."

Cappy let out a string of swearwords and summoning his men, took off down the trail to their horses.

Jake took a deep breath and blew out the air, sounding like one of his mules. He sat shakily down on a boulder. With his head hung low, he sat there and watched the trail where the voices of Pete and Cad would soon produce their bodies around the bend.

Pete had spotted the loaded wagon from the top of the rim as he went for a sheep. Suspecting trouble, he gathered Cad and two other miners who had spent the night at Pete's playing cards, and they took their rifles and headed for Jake's. They stopped by the wagon noticing the load of wood and looked around the area. They spotted the horses tied to the scrub brush and Pete recognized the six men that came running down the hill grabbing the horses and galloping away.

"Now, what the hell do you suppose that was all about, why is the wagon here loaded with wood? Somethin's happened."

"I'm sure I don't know," Cad said once again. He knew the miners were curious but he dared not divulge the plan.

"I know those men, especially that one geezer named Cap Hornaday and his pack of rats. They're the ones who shot up Jake at the mine last year. Jesus, I hope he ain't daid." Pete began to run. He bounded up the steep trail and stopped short before Jake sitting on his boulder.

"What the hell, man, damn it's good to see ya alive. Come on down and let's unload that wagon and put the wood in the ditch. Then after them other two fellers leave, we'll come on up and talk."

Jake rose wearily to his feet. He followed Pete down and together they unloaded the wagon. The other two men bid their farewells and the three men went on up to the stone hut where Jake related the whole story to them.

"Wal, Jake, now what air ya gonna do?" asked Pete.

"I'll tell ya what I'm gonna do, I'm gonna hit my bunk and I'm gonna sleep till noon tomorrow." Jake staggered into the hut and over to his bunk where he flopped down, drew a blanket over his aching body and went promptly to sleep.

CHAPTER EIGHTEEN

THE FOLLOWING DAY Jake and Cad went down to Pete's. Jake had to figure a way to get his gold and get out of there now. Cad had gone into Bodie that night and found the Hornaday gang still there. They did not know who Cad was which allowed him to hang close enough to overhear what was being said. He learned the town's people had told Cappy that they did not think Jake was doing any heavy mining. This information made Cappy decide he was wasting his time, so they headed out for greener pastures.

"Thank you, Cad, for finding all that out for me. It makes me realize I had better do it now or never. I'm worried about the ore in that cave. Someone could stumble upon it just as you did."

Talking it over with Cad and Pete, they decided to have Jake pull out that very afternoon. Preparations were completed and shortly after noon, Jake once more went down the road to the mill.

The trip to the mill was uneventful even though Jake was

highly nervous and sweating profusely. He half expected to see the Hornaday gang ride over the hill after him. He went into the mill and paid the man what he owed him and turned the wagon around toward the hills to where he had his gold in the old cave. The road was no more than a rough trail and travel was difficult. He left the wagon at the bottom of the dry wash where, in the semi-darkness, it would be hard to see, and unhitching the mules, took them up to the cave where he loaded them down heavily. He still had to make another trip to gather it all. Fear of being discovered and ambushed overloaded his imagination so that he felt every little noise was the footstep of death.

Hitching the mules back up, he turned back down the trail toward Carson City. The night had become so dark, he could not see two feet in front of him. He decided he could see better if he got down and led the mules. As it turned out, he made a wrong turn and was off the trail. The wagon bumped along noisily in the night. *Damn*, thought Jake, *I've got to hide somewhere until it gets light enough for me to see.* He pulled off into a small draw and halted.

"Okay, boys, take a break, it's too dark to go any farther. Besides, right now I don't know where the hell I am," he said, patting Blaze on the neck.

He propped himself against the wagon wheel and dozed. He was startled awake by Blaze shifting nervously in his harness. A small breeze had come up and with it an odor that was easy to recognize as rotting meat. Jake sniffed the air. It could be some animal that would make the mules fidgety.

As the first light of dawn appeared over the hills, Jake stood and tried to back the wagon down the way he had come but it was too narrow and overgrown with brush. Large rocks were impeding the wheels so Jake gave up on turning around. The way ahead was almost as bad. He dropped the reins and walked a few feet forward. There was still not enough light to pick out

109

the way clearly. As he moved on ahead, the odor from the night before assailed his nostrils. It was much stronger and seemed to be close by. The scrub willows were thicker and the banks a little steeper. He stumbled and as he fell he saw the foot of a man. He scrambled to his feet as quickly as he could and peering through the gloom, saw the bodies of two men badly decomposed and half eaten by scavengers and buzzards. The smell was awful and the sight worse. Jake gagged and headed back for the mules. No doubt it was the remains of some miners. Possibly even someone he knew. He was going to have to find another way out of there because he sure as hell was not going back that way. It was pretty evident that someone knew this area and he better get the hell out of there fast.

Grabbing Blaze's bridle and turning to the side, he dragged the mules, bumping wildly over rocks and ruts until he finally came to the trail. It wasn't much but it was better by far than what he had just come through. He climbed back into the wagon and took off as fast as the bumpy trail would allow.

The sun was straight up by the time he hit the main trail to Carson City. The going was much easier and Blaze led the mules on at a good fast pace.

Jake was ever watchful for signs of horsemen. He did not like traveling by day but he could not find a suitable place where the wagon could also be hidden. He remembered the ravine where he met Ruth and wondered if the wagon could be put in there. Somehow he either did not recognize it or had passed by, for as the day grew near the end he still had not found a suitable spot. He drew off to the side and spotting some low rising knolls, he headed for them. About fifty feet off the road he stopped and picking some brush, he went back and swept the wagon tracks from sight. He drove the team over behind one knoll where they could not be seen from the road. *Not good, but not bad either*. He did not want to unhitch the mules in case they had to make a fast getaway. Checking each mule over for harness sores, he then gave them a nosebag full of grain.

All seemed well. There was still a good two hours of daylight left and Jake settled down in the wagon to rest. It was pitch-black when he awoke. He took off the nosebags, gave each mule a drink and led them back toward the road, climbed in and headed for Carson City. By the time noon came that day, the country had changed enough for Jake to find adequate protection and he pulled into a small ravine. He gathered brush and covered the wagon so it could not be seen from the road. This time he unhitched the mules and they rolled gratefully in the sand.

The day was miserably hot and he rested in the shade under the wagon. He drowsed peacefully to the sound of nosebag munching. Suddenly, he stiffened! The mules had stopped their eating and with ears pointed, looked up to the top of the ravine. There stood a donkey and a bandy-legged old man with a rifle across his chest.

"Howdy thar," the old man called. "Thought fer a spell thar ya were daid." Taking his donkey by the halter he led it down the ravine. His shifty eyes looked the wagon over carefully and then down at Jake. He stopped short for as he reached Jake, he was looking down the barrel of Jake's rifle.

"Easy thar, son, ain't no reason fer ya ta pull a gun. Ole Mose ain't goin' ta do nothin' to ya, now is he? What'cha got in the wagon that would nervous you up like that?"

He was extremely talkative and kept moving around a lot. Jake kept following him with the rifle, wishing he would stand still. *Damn*, thought Jake, *I have to keep watching him all the time. Can't check out to see if there is anyone else out there.* The old man was almost down to the bottom of the ravine now, working his way around so that the barrel of his gun was pointing in Jake's direction.

Now Blaze raised his head and made little moaning sounds

111

to show his interest in the little donkey. As she hit the bottom of the ravine, Blaze moved out, feed bag and all. In his sudden movement, he ran right over the old man, upsetting and unarming him. Jake slip out from under the wagon and by the time he stood up, had the drop on the old man.

"Now, what was it you're so all fired interested in?" Jake asked.

The old man grinned, stood up dusting himself off. "Wal, now, I was just tryin' to be friendly. You and that gol-dang mule of yers air sure an upsettin' pair." He eyed Jake's deformed body and reached for his rifle.

"Just you leave it lay right there," said Jake as he moved it with his foot. His eyes caught a movement on the ridge of the ravine. He glanced up to see a man reaching for his pistol. Jake fired. Blam! The old man reached for his rifle. Blam! Jake whirled first to one side then to the other. There did not seem to be anyone else around.

He stood with his rifle smoking and shaking in his boots. He hastily filled his rifle and backed against the wagon. He was sure there had to be more of them. Watching the ridge he walked over to where the old man lay and taking the toe of his boot, nudged him over on his back. Jake felt for his pulse, placed his ear over the old man's heart and listened, nothing. He was very dead.

Standing up, he squinted his eyes and tried to locate the man on the ridge he had shot. From where he was, he could not tell if he was lying on the ground or had crawled away. Well, Jake certainly was not going to climb all the way up that ravine to find out if he had done him in or not. He was shaky and sweaty and all he wanted to do was hitch up the mules and be outta there. Reaching in the wagon, he felt for his gun belt and pistol and strapped them on as he glanced around for the mules. Three of the mules were standing peacefully munching their oats. But that gol dang Blaze had followed the little burro down the ravine. He tried to hitch up the other three while holding his gun, watching the ridge and looking for Blaze all at the same time. Blaze had only gone so far and was on his way back by the time Jake had finished harnessing the others.

Jake sighed with relief, put Blaze in his place, took off the nosebag, climbed into the wagon and took off down the ravine toward Carson City.

He was tired, hot and scared as he drove on with his eye peeled for signs of followers. He pushed on for the rest of the day. Jake was upset at the chain of events that kept him out in the open during the day and afforded him little sleep in the early evening. At this rate of travel he would be in Carson City by sometime tomorrow night. By late afternoon he found a good spot to pull into and make camp.

After feeding the mules and eating a small amount of dried meat and cold biscuits, he slept. Rising well before dawn, he hitched the mules and was on his way. The rest of the trip was uneventful and he allowed his mind to drift to thoughts of Ruth.

CHAPTER NINETEEN

LATE THE FOLLOWING evening, he pulled into the Garretts'
yard where he drove on back to the barn, opened the door and
drove in. Unhitching the mules, he climbed back in the wagon
and slept between the sacks of ore.

He was startled awake by the opening of the barn door. Two
of the ranch hands had come in to feed the stock. One he knew
from before but the other one was new. He was tall and slender
with small beady black eyes and an alert air. Jake felt he was
not to be trusted.

Matt spoke to Jake. "Gawd damn, Jake, ya sure gave me a
turn. Didn't even hear ya come in. What time did ya get here
anyway?"

"Late last night, Matt. How's it goin'?"

"Not so good, Jake, the old man died here a couple of weeks
ago and some geezer in town seems ta be tryin' ta take the
ranch away from the missus."

"What do you mean, Matt? Take the ranch away, how could
he do that?"

"I really don't know much about it. You see, the mister died while I was away visiting my family. I just got back a short while ago and that's all I heard."

"Hmmm!" muttered Jake, stroking his beard and looking at the younger man who seemed to be awfully interested in what was in his wagon. "What's the matter there, young fella, got a case of nose trouble?"

"Not really, just lookin'."

"Yeah, so I noticed." He gave Jake an uneasy feeling, like maybe he better get hitched up and head on in to Carson City and the assay office. He knew Sarah would be up and fixing breakfast for the boarders and would probably hear him leave, but first things first. He could wait there until the assay office opened.

He pulled around to the side yard, tied up the team and strolled around to the front. From there he could watch both the street and the wagon.

The rapid staccato of approaching hooves caused Jake to glance up at the rider as he turned into the side street. Through the glare of the early morning sun, he thought he recognized the man as the new hand from the Garrett ranch. *Now what's he doing here this early in the morning,* he thought, *if that was really him.* He strained his eyes waiting but the rider did not appear again. *Hmmm!* thought Jake. *Wonder where he went?*

The sun flipped over the desert rim like a copper penny, stirring the residents to begin their day. One could hear the hammer of some industrious individual on the street behind and the smell of bacon frying assaulted Jake's nose with a beckoning finger. Wagons were rolling down the street, their harnesses creaking. Two young boys came running down the walkway, shouting and laughing, and at that moment the manager of the assay office, his keys jangling, opened his doors. "Good morning. You're bright and early this morning. Been waiting long?"

"No, sir, not too long. Didn't mind the wait though, morning's the best time of day to be alive. Kinda enjoyed its pleasures."

The ore, although it did not carry the weight of the first, had a value of $25,000 a ton. His load weighed in at a little over a half a ton.

After the wagon was unloaded and Jake had deposited his money, he drove the wagon over to the blacksmith where the young crippled boy, Paul, came running up to meet him.

"Hey there, Jake, sure good ta see ya again. Where ya been? I thought when ya bought them mules you'd be around ta see me again."

"Hello, Paul. Well, it's a little hard for me to come see you, boy. I live many miles from here. By the way, I sure want to thank you for putting me on to those two mules, best pair of animals I ever owned."

"Thought you'd like them. It makes me feel good that they got a good home with somebody who would care for them. What ya need this time?"

"I'm looking for a good wagon this time. This one is coming apart."

Paul climbed up into the wagon and looking the bed over, picked up a small nugget that had broken loose from some ore. "What did ya carry in this wagon, gold?"

"Yep! Now, about that wagon?"

"Gold, really? Where ya been? Did ya get much of the stuff? Is there any more out there where ya come from? How much did the stuff weigh? I never knew anyone who struck it rich before. Lookie, here's another little piece."

Jake sighed. "Please, Paul, the wagon? Do ya have a wagon for sale? Where's the blacky?"

"He's up at the café having breakfast. I'll show ya where the wagons are and while yer lookin' at them, I'll go get the blacky."

116

Jake looked at the three wagons lined up behind the barn. One was not much more than a small springboard, the other was not in much better condition than the one he had, but the third was a sturdy double bottom wagon that looked pretty good. Upon investigation, Jake could see some definitely good advantages to that double bottom. Jake bought the wagon, hitched the mules to it and prepared to leave.

"Wait, Jake, could I ride with ya as far as the edge of town? I could walk back. Please?"

"Okay, son, hop on."

They headed out of town and as they passed the assay office, Jake noticed two men emerge onto the boardwalk from around the corner of the building. One stopped abruptly and backed around the corner again but the man in gray came on as if he was not a party to the other man, eyes straight ahead.

Ah yes, there was the man in gray again. Mr. Lord, the friendly undertaker. But it was the man who backed around the corner that interested Jake most, but by the time Jake reached the corner he had vanished.

Paul looked back over his shoulder at Mr. Lord. "Boy, I sure hate that bastard. He's mean and underhanded."

"What do you know of that man, Paul?"

"Well, not too much. I do know that he has a band of outlaws that meet him every so often down in the livery stable. Sometimes Cecil, the fella that takes care of Mr. Lord's team and buggy, goes into town and goes on a toot. He always asks me to spend the night in the loft so I can watch out for things while he's gone. Seems like every time I do, there is some kind of meetin' with that bunch. Everyone in town suspects him of some kind of dirty work but they would be surprised if they knew what I know."

"Like what?" asked Jake.

"Like he plans holdups of gold trains from different places. And he's always doin' some poor widower out of her money and land. He's the only undertaker in town so he gets in on all the easy marks. Cecil says he's workin' on someone now."

"Where do you get all your information, Paul? Do you eavesdrop on everyone's conversations?"

"People think I'm just a poor old crippled orphan boy and don't know nothin'. Boy, do I have news fer them." Paul put his hand over his mouth and giggled.

"You know, Paul, you could be a great help to me, if you would. I would like for you to keep a close ear open on their conversations. I will be coming back to Carson City in the near future and I would be interested in all you have heard. Maybe we can put a kink in a few of his wheels. Will you do that for me?"

"You bet I will, if that means I'll get to see you again. Here's where I get off. Thanks for the ride, Jake, and I'll do as you ask."

"Good-bye, Paul, and thank you."

As Jake turned into the Garrett ranch, the young man with the beady eyes was coming around the corner of the bunkhouse. *Well, I'll be danged. I guess the fellow I saw in town couldn't be him, I swear it sure looked like him.*

As Jake unhitched the mules and took them out to the corral behind the barn he noticed a small two-stall shed, and as he approached, he heard the munching of grain. Cautiously he opened the door. There, all lathered and steaming, stood the horse he had seen in town. *Man, he must have ridden the shoes off this mare to have gotten there, done his business and get back before me. Now, why should anyone be doing this over him?* It was pretty obvious to Jake that this man was in cahoots with Mr. Lord and probably knew all about him and his gold teeth. Perhaps he had ridden in to warn Mr. Lord, which meant pushing the little mare both ways. *I have a feeling that the predator who is trying to take Sarah's land is that sanitary freak. If so, what does this ranch have that would be of so much interest to a man like that? Think I'd better stick around for a while and do a little investigating.*

He walked into the bunkhouse, drew himself a pan full of hot water from the stove, washed and put on clean clothes. He headed for the ranch house, opened the door and stopped short. Did he hear a baby crying? He listened. Yes, he did, what...? Just at that moment Sarah burst through the kitchen door.

"Jake, land sakes, son, but it's good to see ya." She engulfed him with her plump arms. "Thought I heard ya leave here a few hours back. Was I right? Where were ya aheadin' at that time in the mornin'? Seems like there were a lot of comin' and goin' around here early this morning."

"What do you mean, Sarah? What kind of coming and going?"

"Wal, I heard you leave, I knew it was you 'cause I looked. Then that new fella we just hired rode outta here like his tail was on fire, then pretty soon he came back the same way, really pushin' that little mare of his."

"Something funny is going on here, Sarah. While I was down at the assay office, I could of swore I saw that fellow ride into town, but it was still not pure daylight yet and I was not sure. Later, Mr. Lord came out on the walkway with another man who, when he saw me, ducked back behind the building. He also looked like your young hired man. But when I returned home I saw him walking toward the ranch house just like he always had been here. Then when I turned the mules out in the back corral, I noticed the two-stall shed you have and I played a hunch and went down there. There she was, that little lathered up mare. Do you have any idea where he came from? How long has he been working here? Matt told me about Fred's death and that someone was trying to take the ranch. Who is he and what makes him think he has any right to the ranch?"

"Lord, Jake, one thing at a time. First, yes, Fred did die here two weeks ago. As you know, Fred has been ailin' a good many

119

years. He never did give up the thought he would get well and take to runnin' the ranch again. Without me knowin' it, he had been borrowin' sums of money off and on. Well, borrowin' is one thing, payin' back is another. I don't know why the bank loaned him so much money. They knew he was sick. I know most of the money went fer doctor bills but there was considerable more borrowed than that. Anyway, this Mr. Lord you speak of, somehow bought up all the promissory notes from the bank and now he's the one we owe money to.

"And he wants the money by sundown this very day or he will foreclose on the ranch. Now, for land sakes, I don't know what he wants with this place. It sure ain't the kind of a place a man like him would want. This is dirt farmin' and ranchin' and he'd get his pretty white gloves dirty. Now where are we gonna come up with money like that by sundown today? Oh, and by the way, Mr. Lord sent that new man out to us. Told us to hire him 'cause he could use the work and we needed another man. I wasn't much fer it but I didn't seem to have much of a choice."

"This whole thing smells," grumbled Jake. "How much money do you owe, Sarah?"

"All told, Jake, it amounts to $2,500 and it might just as well be $25,000. There ain't enough stock or equipment to raise half that amount. If I were to let the hired hand go, only got two anymore, and took in more boarders, sold the stock, then maybe I could pay off the man in time, but he won't even let me try. Seems like he's pushin fer this property."

"Hmmm! The more I think about it, the more I can see the advantages this place could offer. It's only half a mile from town and the town's growing this way. It could offer a good front to some illegal dealings, be far enough from town to hold down suspicions, yet close enough to get there fast if needs be. He probably has something up his sleeve."

Just then the door opened and Ruth came through carrying

a baby. Jake started slightly, recovering, he drawled, "Mornin', Ruth."

"Oh, Jake, it's so good to see you. I never heard from you in all these months, I was afraid something happened to you." She walked over to where he stood and placed a hand on his arm. Jake stared at the baby sleeping in her arms, a small infant of perhaps a month or so old. She smiled and said, "Yes, Jake, mine. Ralph Dove's and mine. If he had not been killed, we would have been a family. Strange, I knew him for so short a time and now I can hardly remember him at all. Look at her, Jake, isn't she beautiful?"

Jake just stood there trembling. She reached out and took his arms, placing the baby in them. Jake was petrified. He had never held a baby before and was afraid he would drop her. Ruth gave a tinkling laugh and reached for the baby. "I've named her after Aunt Sarah, Jake, Sarah May. Isn't that a pretty name?" Jake agreed. He would have agreed to anything at that point. She was so beautiful and poor Jake's heart was about to burst. She turned, kissed Sarah and returned to her room.

"Lord, Jake, she's like a gift from heaven. She's always happy, always seein' the bright side of everything. She says her life till now has been such pure hell that she now lives in heaven and people in heaven are always happy. Here, boy, sit down and have some coffee while I talk to ya. I'll fix ya some breakfast while I'm talkin'.

"Fred took sick shortly after ya left last November. Had a real bad time of it. Kept goin' into a coma, then comin' out of it. Went on like that fer months. I don't know what I would a done without that girl. She nursed him just like he was her own pa. She's an angel, Jake, why don't ya tell her how ya feel? Give her a chance."

"Give her a chance, my God, Sarah! What kind of a chance does a beautiful young girl like her have with an ugly old bastard like me? Look at me, Sarah! I'm ugly! Do you see, ugly!" He began pacing the floor waving his arms and raving, "Ugly! I never hated my body so much before. Even if it were not for my deformed body, I'm old enough to be her father. Now, what kind of a chance is that for a young girl?"

Sarah smiled. "But she does care fer ya, Jake."

"No, she does not, only as someone who has been kind to her."

Jake poured himself another cup of coffee and walked to the window. "Tell me, Sarah, how did it go with Ruth? I mean, with the baby? Is she happy? What is she going to do about the baby?"

"Well, Jake, I guess I was just as surprised about the baby as anyone. But with her type of past, the only way she could get out of that sort of life was to get pregnant, which she did. She and Ralph Dove became afraid when Duke claimed the coming baby was his'n, that's what made them decide to take the chance of runnin' away. As you know, that didn't work. Ruth spent a happy winter here with us.

"We had an old man with us here fer a short spell that used to be a school teacher and he spent most of his time teachin' Ruth to read and write. She spent a lot of her time studyin', she's real proud of being able to read some. The baby was born around the middle of May and she had a fairly easy time of it. Named the mite after me, made me feel proud. We talked a lot this winter, her and me, and she told me many things about her life. 'Course, we talked about ya a lot too, Jake, only I don't know much about ya or yer past. Ruth said she had takin' a liken' to ya and hoped and prayed ya would come back again soon. Now yer here, why don't ya pay some mind to the girl? She needs it."

Jake sighed, he just could not make this woman understand how wrong it was to court the girl. His age and body were against him but he could not still his pounding heart. A plan was forming in his mind as he stood there listening to Sarah talk. He would go into Carson City and draw up a will, a large portion of his money now on deposit in the bank would become Ruth's and the baby's upon his death. Even though she might be married to someone at the time, it would still become hers. Jake turned from the window to face Sarah. Sarah, I want you to stop playing matchmaker between Ruth and me. I'm sure any feeling she had for me is due to your constant talk about me, you've stimulated this feeling she has for me."

Just as he finished his sentence, they heard the sound of horses and buggy wheels coming up the lane. Hurrying to the front window, they spotted a perfectly matched team of dappled gray horses trotting in front of a black buggy.

"Oh, good Lord, it's Mr. Lord," quipped Sarah. "Now what does he want out here at this time of mornin'?"

As the team pulled to a stop, Jake said, "I want to stay out of sight and hear what he says, so I'll go in the sitting room there." Jake retreated around the corner just as there was a rap at the back door.

"Good morning, Mrs. Garrett. I see that you have not gathered your things together, that must mean you have the money."

"No, I ain't got the money. Why cain't ya just let me have the time I need to raise the money? You weren't pressuring Mr. Garrett this way. Why cain't ya let me be?"

"Now, you know perfectly well, Mr. Garrett and I had one kind of deal, and you and I have another. I told you I wanted my money by today or for you to be out. Now I come here and find you have neither moved nor do you have the money. I will give you people till noon to have your things out and off the property. Those things which remain here at noon will be confiscated by me, for my disposal."

"Now that will be about all," said Jake as he came around the corner from the sitting room. "Here is your money, all of it and a little more. You take it and get, you bastard. You low down dirty bastard. Here, Sarah, take this and pay the son-of-a-bitch off. We'll talk our terms later."

Mr. Lord's face turned red, he squinted his eyes at Jake as he reached into his breast pocket and drew out the promissory notes and not even removing his gloves, signed them PAID IN FULL. As he handed the notes back to Sarah, he glowered at Jake. "You hairy, hunched, deformed little freak, sweet revenge will be mine." Clapping his gloved hands together, he turned on his heels and slammed out the door.

"I'm afraid you've made yerself a dangerous enemy, Jake. I'm sure he could do ya much harm if he set his mind to it. I understand he controls several gangs of evil men. He could even reach you in Bodie. You'd best be careful."

The sting of Mr. Lord's cruel words were still with him. Yes, he'd better close off his dealings here and head back home sooner than he had planned. He now had to go back into town and draw out some more money, pick up the things from the pharmacist that Cad wanted and move on out.

That evening after the meal was finished and the kitchen cleaned, Ruth came to Jake and asked, "Jake, would you walk with me?" Jake looked at her, heaved a sigh and nodded his head. She beamed at him and ran to get her shawl.

They took the lane out past the barn and as they came to the corral, Blaze gave a squeaky bray to Jake and sauntered over to the fence. They stopped and Ruth put her hand on the mule's nose. "My, Jake, he is sure red, I've never seen one so pretty before. And he's so big, bigger than a horse." She scratched him under his chin and Blaze leaned his head against her. "Oh, Jake, he's a love. I didn't know mules were so lovable."

"Well, Ruth, honey, I think he's more human than mule. Sometimes he's a gol dang pest, and at other times—well, I don't know what I'd do without him."

He reached over and gave the mule a pat and scratched him behind the ears. Blaze leaned heavily against the man's hand encouraging more scratching.

They moved on down the lane, strolling slowly, making the most of time. "Tell me, Jake, how are things in Bodie? Do you ever see Duke and his men? Is it still as wild? Is Madam Rosie still working her girls?"

"Hold on, Ruth, one question at a time. First, yes, Rosie is still working her girls and no, I haven't seen Duke or his men. I hear he's in Arizona and I hope he stays there. And Bodie is still wild, maybe even a little wilder. It just keeps on growing, with all the wrong kind of people." He went on telling her about Cad and his misadventures.

Ruth laughed and agreed that he would probably end up with his head blown off. Jake also told her about Pete Dunning and how they planned his getaway this time. They walked and talked until dusk set in.

As they approached the barn, Ruth put her hand on Jake's arm and looked at him. "Jake, I want to thank you for all you've done for me. I don't know what I would have done without your kindness. You're truly one of the kindest and most decent men I know." She moved in close to him and put her lips on his.

Jake could not stop the pounding of his heart and he trembled at the touch of her lips. "Ruth, honey, you must not treat me so, it is not fair for I care too much and I cannot take the chance on your caring for me. I'm a crippled up old man where you are concerned. You are young and beautiful and should set your eyes on a nice young fellow who could care for you and the baby."

"But Jake, I do care for you. Won't you please kiss me? You are forcing me to become a shameless hussy by having to ask you."

Jake could not resist her plea. He put his arms around her and held her close. "Ruth, honey, you cannot know how much I care." He kissed her hard, putting all his love into that kiss.

He drew away from her and spoke huskily. "Now, Ruth, please do not torment me anymore for I cannot join my life with yours. It would not be right for you. Can you not understand? I'm an ugly, deformed man, old enough to be your father."

"Oh, but Jake, I do not care. Can't I make you understand?"

"No, Ruth, I cannot do such a thing to you."

She reached out and put her arms around his neck, placing her body up against him. "Please kiss me again, Jake."

He kissed her and held her close, rocking gently to and fro. He put up a hand and stroked her hair. Shakily he loosened the pins until it flowed loose about her shoulders. He ran his fingers through the golden strands and placed them over his own shoulders until he was covered with her hair. Tears dimmed his eyes and he fell to kissing her once again. "Oh, my God, Ruth, I love you so. This night will be my one living memory for the rest of my life. I shall feel your arms, your kisses, and smell the cleanness of your hair in my dreams."

Finally he pushed her from him. "This is enough, Ruth, I can't take much more. I simply will not let you ruin yourself by attaching your life with mine. Now we'll talk no more about it. Come, let's go back to the house."

CHAPTER TWENTY

THE BEAUTY OF the morning was lost on Jake as he made the return trip to Bodie. His heart was sore and he was drowning in memories of Ruth. It was hard to leave without telling her good-bye, but he knew he would find it harder if he had to listen to her plead for him to stay. The night before was all the memory he needed, he did not need a memory of tears.

As he came down off a ridge of low mountains, Jake could see smoke. It appeared to be a brush fire. As he neared the area, he turned south but found the fire to be wide spread, blocking off both trails. He pulled up the mules and stared out over the desert. He either had to find a way through or go many miles out of his way. He didn't want another bout with wildfire like the three of them had gone through a few weeks back. *This is getting to be a habit*, Jake thought. There was a burned over space between the two trails and Jake forged ahead. The mules were becoming fidgety and balky. Suddenly a spur of fire blazed up and burned toward them in a northern direction. Jake pulled the wagon around and headed southwest. He would have to leave the road and bump along until he could get around the spur. The winds were blowing hot and hard, smoke filled the air and choked off their breath.

He tried to hurry, yet control the mules. They wanted to go all different directions and no matter which way he went, the winds blew the fire in his direction so rapidly he could not get away. Pounding hooves, bumping wagon and air filled with smoke almost made Jake miss the large pile of rocks ahead. If he could get there, maybe the fire would burn around him. He raced the mules, bumping wildly across the smoking ground. He made the rock pile and jumping from the wagon, ran up between the two lead mules. Grabbing their bridles, he pulled their heads down and true to form, Blaze sat. This was good for it quieted the rest.

Wind, smoke and fire billowed over their heads and around both sides. The heat was fierce and almost more than Jake could bear. He coughed and gagged. The mules were gasping and heaving.

Oh, God, thought Jake, *what a way to die!* He slipped into unconsciousness.

Awareness came slowly. He groaned, opened his eyes to see the mules standing quietly and the air much less smoky. Ashes covered everything. Jake, wagon, mules and ground were covered with it. Jake got to his feet and climbed to the top of the rock pile. The road through the fire was clear now. It ran like a ribbon through a black sea. He got down and pulled Blaze to his feet, climbed into the wagon and wearily turned the team toward Bodie and home.

A quarter mile or so down the road Jake came across the remains of two wagons. Studying the situation, it appeared the fire might have started from here. Blackened pots still hung over a dead pit. The charcoal remains of many bodies could be seen here and there. The fierce desert winds must have caught the campfire and spread it across the dry desert. Somehow it must have turned back on them, at least that was how it looked, otherwise how could they have been caught?

It was a horrible sight and Jake was not about to get down and look for more, it was sickening enough from there. He moved on a few yards, then stopped. There was something strange about all this. He turned around in the wagon and looked back...yes, that was it. Where were the animals? There had to be teams to draw the wagons. He looked around becoming uneasy. The hair stood up on the back of his neck and his skin crawled.

He urged the tired mules to a trot and moved out, keeping watch on all sides of him. In a very short time he was out of the blackened area but the uneasiness did not leave him. The hours went by and dusk began to settle down around them. He turned the mules up a small ravine and stopped, turning the wagon around so he could get out fast, then settled down in the wagon to sleep, not even unhitching the mules. But sleep evaded him and somewhere in the middle of the night came the sound he had been expecting, the sound of muffled hooves. The night was extremely dark and if the mules would keep quiet, he would not be detected.

Suddenly a light pushed the darkness back and a lantern held by a man who was leading a mule came into view. There were several more men following him and a wagon or two behind them. He heard a voice call, "Hey, boys, here's a good place."

Jake panicked, good God, they were going to pile in on him and there would sure be a hell of a fight. He was just about to make a run for it and ride right over them. The element of surprise might serve him here. But to Jake's surprise, the man with the lantern turned into the ravine to the left of the road. Jake was shaking with relief. He was amazed that Blaze or one of the other mules did not bray out a welcome to the new arrivals. Now, if they would just keep the peace, he might get by.

The men and wagons turned up the opposite ravine and began making preparations to camp.

Wonderful! Jake thought. *How in the hell am I gonna get out of here without being seen or heard? Come daylight and I'm staring at them straight in the face. If one of their mules brayed, mine would probably all answer him. Then I'm a goner.* The night dragged on. Soon a man on horseback joined the group. "Say there, Vic, what took ya so long?"

"Found out somethin', boys, seems there was some feller in Bodie that's responsible fer settin' them Chinese loose. Looks like we're gonna have ta go back to Bodie and find out who that feller is. The big boss ain't gonna set fer somebody tamperin' with his plans. If we don't find out who it is and finish him, Mr. Lord will."

Mr. Lord! thought Jake. *Am I never going to hear the end of that man? He must have a hand into every crime in the west.* Jake pulled at his beard, a little worm of worry wandered through his mind. The "feller" in Bodie who turned the Chinese free, could it possibly be Cad? Jake sighed, yes, it very possibly could be. If Cad was running true to form, that would be just up his creek. *Wonder what the heck these men were doing in Bodie with Chinese anyway. From what I remember of Vic and his gang of morons, he was working some kind of wild religious game. That is, until he got tangled up with some Gypsy troupe.* Jake chuckled to himself as he remembered how they plagued him for months with some kind of magic tricks until they got him so superstitious, he was afraid of his own shadow.

Hmmm! That gives me an idea. Climbing in the back of the wagon, he found an old burlap sack. Taking his bowie knife, he cut it to shreds, then ripped a hole in it for his head. He then rubbed it against the mules until he had it black with soot. *Now, what else can I do to this?* He held it up, stroking his beard as he thought. *Blood, that's what I need. But where am I going to get blood? I could cut the vein in the neck of one of the mules*

130

*like they do when you bleed them for blood disorders, but it's
so dark I'm afraid to chance it. Maybe if I struck a match back
by the back two mules, their bodies would shield the flame. I
think I will.* The match flared and no one saw it and one quick
stroke of the knife severed the vein.

Placing the blood-soaked, blackened sack over his head, and
smearing blood all over his face and hands, he led the team out
to the road.

Someone crossed the road and shoved a lantern into Jake's
face. Jake slowly raised his arms above his head, uttering a
wavering unholy sound.

"Ahhhhhhhgeeee! Aghhhh! Whooooee!"

"Jesus Christ! Vic, God damn, Vic—look at him. He's the
devil, he is, look at that hunched back and him drippin' with
blood. The demons, they done caught up with us, jest like that
Gypsy woman said they would. Done raised from the grave, he
did. Augh! I ain't stayin' ta see what he wants." The fellow
dropped the lantern and fled.

Vic came slowly forward, picked up the lantern and
cautiously raised it to better see Jake. His face contorted. "It's
true, the Gypsy curse has come true."

Jake played it for all it was worth. He lunged and with a
wavering voice said, "The black curse is upon you. The winds
of the demons shall blow across the desert and into the gates of
hell."

Vic staggered back in fear. Jake raised his arms in a vulture-
like manner and hissed through his teeth, "You shall die, all of
you shall die for I have placed the black curse of death upon
you. Whoooooeeee!"

"Augh! Augh!" screamed Vic. "Move on out, men, hurry,
move on out. Quick, let's get the hell outta here." In the
distance lightning flashed, heralding the approach of a summer
storm. It seemed to accent Jake's performance and the party
scurried around in panic to depart.

Dawn was upon them as Jake pulled the team out into the road and the horizon was black with thunderheads. Jake stood threateningly in the middle of the road backed up by a team of soot-blackened mules. The whole episode tickled Jake and he guffawed happily after they left.

"Blaze, old mule, that was one payback I surely enjoyed." He patted the mule and walked back to check on the mule he had cut. The bleeding had stopped long ago and dried on his coat. "Time to go home, boys."

As they traveled on, Jake let his mind dwell on Vic and his gang. I wonder what they were up to. I have a feeling they were the ones responsible for the fire. And while I'm worryin' I might just as well try to guess what Cad has been up to, that scares me.

By the time he reached Bodie he was a mess—fire, soot, blood, rain, wind and dust. God, what a trip.

He pulled into Pete's place, everyone came running out—stopped short and stared. He unhitched with Pete's help. "Lordy, Jake, and I presume it is Jake I'm atalkin' to, you all air a terrible mess."

Jake nodded, backed Blaze until he sat, straddled his back, gave him a kick and headed down the road for home. Somewhere at the bottom of the hill he began to strip. By the time he reached the hut he was almost naked.

Turning the mules loose and grabbing the huge tub, he went indoors. Cad was not there. Stoking the fire to a roaring blaze, he heated a bucket of water and poured it into the tub, filling it the rest of the way with cool water and slid into the tepid water with a sigh.

While Jake was soaking in the tub, the door opened and Jake, expecting to see Cad, found himself face to face with a Chinese boy. The startled Chinese jumped and produced a knife from within his sleeve.

"Now, just you hold on a minute. This happens to be my

house, my tub, and you happen to be the intruder here."

The boy dropped his arm and smiled, bowed his head and said, "You must be Mr. Jake. Mr. Cad, my friend, I his houseboy, Lin Chu. Lin Chu cook, wash, clean, and dig for gold. Lin Chu Jake's friend too, yes?"

"Oh no, Gawd damn it! Where's that feeble-minded nitwit anyway? What the hell's he usin' for brains? Get the hell outta here and let me get dressed."

Lin Chu made a dash for the towel and held it for Jake. "No, sir! No, sir! No Chinese houseboy is gonna dry me off. Now, I said for you to get the hell outta here and that's just what I meant." He picked up the soap and hurled it across the room at Lin Chu who retreated through the door at great speed. Jake grabbed the towel and mumbling to himself, began to dry off.

"When I get a hold of Cad, I'm gonna kill him before somebody else does. Now where in the hell do you suppose he picked up that boy?"

He dressed and went outside where Lin Chu stood unhappily with his hands tucked into his sleeves and knees shaking.

Jake's heart filled with pity. He could understand the pain of nonacceptance the boy was feeling. It was no stranger to him. He put his hand on Lin Chu's shoulder and said, "I'm sorry, boy, but you startled me. I just ain't used to having some man walk in on me and I sure ain't used to being waited on. Now, do you know where Cad is?"

Lin Chu smiled and nodded. "Mr. Cad down at Mr. Pete's. He happy, free all my family. Bad man burn wagons, many friends die, all my family die, fire go all over desert. Lin Chu find road, follow back to Mr. Cad. No place for Lin Chu to go."

Jake looked long at the Chinese boy. This explained the fire, all the burned wagons and the people. A sudden fear welled up in Jake's stomach. "Lin Chu, I haven't had a proper meal since I left Carson City. See if you can rustle up some grub and I'll go fetch Cad." Lin Chu smiled and nodding his head, hurried back into the shack to comply with Jake's wishes.

Jake took off for Pete's. Cad would know by now he was back and he wondered where he was when he came in earlier.

Just as he reached the bottom of the hill, Cad rounded the corner on his way home, his face showing pain and fear. It was obvious he had heard from Lin Chu the fate of the people he had tried so hard to save.

"Jake, oh, thank God you're home. Something terrible has happened and I'm directly to blame. I doubt I shall ever get over it. The whole Potter family and all. Oh, my God, my God." He sat down in the middle of the road and put his hands over his face. "Pete said I'm not to blame because I couldn't know what would happen, but I am, Jake, I am."

"Now, now, Cad, come on home. Lin Chu is fixin' something to eat and you can tell me all about it." They walked back to the shack and Cad and Lin Chu told this story while they ate...

CHAPTER TWENTY-ONE

ON THE DAY Jake left for Carson City, Cad went into Bodie and spent the day in town. While having a drink in the Nugget Saloon, he heard a ruckus outside and wandered out to see what was going on. There was a band of cutthroats with a few mules and wagons dragging a chain. Attached to the chain were about twenty to thirty hot, dusty and tired Chinese men.

The troop stopped in front of the saloon and lining the men up at a horse trough, ordered them to drink. Cad watched with his mouth open. How could one man be so cruel to another man even though he was not of the same color? In the wagon were, perhaps, a dozen women and several children. The driver and some of the other men went into the saloon for a drink.

Cad followed them in. They stood at the bar and some of the local men started asking questions. They were, they said, on the way to the railroad with the Chinese people where they would sell them for workers.

Cad walked outside. The Chinese were squatting in the middle of the road. He gingerly walked around them and peered into the wagon. The wagon was hot and the women looked miserable. Cad walked across the street to the café and brought back a pitcher of cold water and several cups to the wagon. The women just sat there and stared at him.

"Go ahead, drink," said Cad.

One older man got up and came over to the wagon. He spoke to the women in Chinese and they reached gratefully for the water. He then spoke to Cad. "The people of my country have been treated cruelly by the Americans. They do not trust you but I do. You have been kind to us and should you need help, you can know we'll help you."

Cad's eyes dimmed, he could not understand how men could treat other men so cruel.

There was quite a crowd gathering to look at the drooping Chinese men. Cad began inspecting the chain that bound them. If there were only some way he could loosen it. Each man wore leg irons with a stretch of chain attached, on the end was a ring and through those rings ran a long chain, at the end was a T-bar and bolt.

An idea was forming. He wandered back into the saloon and leaning his arms on the bar, asked for a drink, then turned so that he was half facing the men and listened to their conversation. Finally he spoke. "Say, how long you gonna be here clutterin' up the street with them Chinks?"

"Wal, now, ain't we smart mouthed?" spoke up one of the men. "Suppose I told ya it was none of yer Gawd damn business? Then what would ya say?"

"I'd say, you could stay all you wanted to but you'd better get those Chinks off the street before somethin' happens. People are all over them out there and everybody's gettin' restless."

The man bolted for the door. "Hey, get away from them slaves. Do ya wanna' get yer throats cut? Hey, Mike, come on, let's go park this rig somewhere and come back."

The fellow called Mike gulped down the rest of his drink and spoke to his partner. "Be right back, man, so keep my spot warm and be on the lookout fer a pretty gal or two, I'm gettin' hot."

Cad walked to the door and watched. They made a wide swing and headed downhill to the livery stable. *Good*, thought Cad. He followed a short distance back and saw that they pulled on out of town a short distance and parked in the shade of a few outbuildings. Then, laughing and slapping each other on the arm, they headed back to the saloon.

Cad waited for a spell, then walked over to the general store where he purchased a hacksaw, a file and a hunk of cheese. He then slipped down to where the Chinese slaves were and dumping the purchases in the wagon, took the hacksaw and began sawing the end of the bolt.

Walking back to the older Chinese men, he said, "Now, when you get out from town about four hours, the bolt will drop and you start dropping off. There will be a family with three wagons waiting out there and as soon as you get loose and take your women from the wagons, they will pick you up. You will then have to jump those men so they can't come after you again. The Potters will do what they can to help you find your freedom."

The older man seemed to be the spokesman for the group. "I thank you, my friend. We will prepare ourselves for the escape."

As Cad started to leave, one of the older boys stopped him. He bowed eloquently, saying, "I you friend, I look you up." He nodded his head, hands folded inside his sleeves.

Cad stared. "You can't, boy, they'd find you and kill you."

"No find Lin Chu, he be with friend, they no catch, no kill. Good friend take care of Lin Chu. Lin Chu take good care of friend. I his house boy."

Cad stood back and looked at the boy. Well, once out there

with the rest of them, he would no doubt change his mind. He was sure the older man would see to it. He turned and walked back home.

The wagons, mules, men and slaves all moved out of town in the early hours before dawn. They were on the road only a short time when the T-bar fell off. It was far too early to start the drop off and they found it difficult for the end ones to stay hooked on. They labored as long as they could and finally started the drop off. Somewhere out there was the Potter family waiting for them. Everything was going fine until one of the younger children began to cry.

"Hey, Gawd damn it, cain't you women shut that brat up?" one of the men hollered as he dropped back. He stopped short! "Hey Vic, Vic, Gawd damn it, man, hold up. Somethin's wrong." The sun was climbing ever closer to the top of the hills giving considerably more light to see by. "Jesus, man, the Chinese have broken loose. Thar's only four left."

The Chinese men began their attack. They only had fists and a few sticks to fight with. The men were on horseback and had the advantage, kicking and beating at their heads. Several of the Chinese were attempting to get the women and children out of the wagon. When Vic saw what they were doing, he screamed, cursed and shot off his gun. That was the worse thing he could have done for it startled the mules drawing the wagon, who took off bucking and braying across the countryside. The Chinese scattered and Vic and his men had to take off across the desert after the mules.

The Chinese gathered off to the right in a small gully and waited for Vic and his gang to be gone, then started the long walk looking for the Potter wagons. Every so often one of the men would climb up to the road and scan the horizon for sign of the Potters or the gang.

It was almost noon when they spotted the Potter wagons and they all ran yelling and cheering. The Potters greeted them warmly and helped the women and children into one of the wagons. They ate a hurried lunch as they moved along toward Carson City.

As darkness approached they were almost to the junction to Carson City when Vic and his men overtook them.

"Okay, all of you, put yer hands in the air and just stand thar." They hurried to obey. "Now, Bill, you just unhitch them mules and bring them over here."

Bill got down and unhitched the mules as Vic told his men to unhitch the front mules. Vic then reached for the other two and as he did, he turned and started shooting. The men gathered all the mules and headed back toward Bodie. They were to wait for Vic further down the road and he would bring back the Chinese so they could go on with their business. Vic continued shooting, massacring almost everyone. One of the Chinese men, when shot, fell backwards onto fire, scattering fir and embers all over the ground. Some of the brush started to burn and the strong winds spread it rapidly. Those strong heat-driven winds blew in erratic directions circling around to double back and catch afire all that were in its path.

Lin Chu took a deep breath and said, "Lin Chu ran away fast. Come back to friend. No hear from the others."

The rest of the story was Jake's and he gave everyone a much needed laugh.

CHAPTER TWENTY-TWO

THE FOLLOWING DAY Jake left Lin Chu and Cad at the shack and headed for Pete's place. He found the family in conference in the shade of a canvas lean-to. He stopped short, not wanting to intrude.

"Come on over, Jake, this is about you and Cad anyhow." Jake went over and sat down. Pete reached up and scratched his head as he spoke. "Now, Jake, what in hell air we gonna do about Cad?"

"I don't know, Pete, the worst is yet to come, I'm afraid." Jake then related his part of the story and his fears that the three men were already in Bodie.

"Wal, now, that puts a different light on it. I can plainly see that with Lin Chu around, Cad is in real trouble. Fer a man of his education, he sure ain't got any horse sense."

"I'm afraid you're right, Pete."

"We're all a talkin' and figured it's time we pulled outta these parts. Been shippin' some of my gold and having the funds transferred to Texas. 'Course, I'm sure some of that gold never made it to the assay office so I don't rightly know how much funds ever reached Texas. I figure on loaden' that false bottom wagon down with the rest. Right now, we gotta wait 'cause Clara is sick with the fever again and we don't want to travel until she is well enough to go."

Jake stood and stared at Pete, his voice cracked as he said, "I hate ta see you go, Pete. You're the only friend I have here in Bodie. You ask me what we're gonna do about Cad. Well, I'd like to tie him up and send him off with you, but..."

"Oh no, ya don't," Pete hollered, "I ain't gonna take that stupid son-of-a-bitch with me to Texas. I'd probably kill him afore we got there anyway."

Jake broke down and laughed, it was hysterical the way Cad affected Pete even though some days Pete seemed to tolerate Cad rather well. "I've been thinking, Pete, about going on into Bodie myself but they'd spot me for sure. And if you went, it's sure as hell you'd never recognize them. I guess I'll have to chance it, I've gotta find out what they're up to now."

"Reckon yer the only one, save Cad, that knows what they look like. But chances are, even if they do recognize you, they'd be more apt to be afeared of you than anything else, seein' as how you scared the livin' hell outta them."

Jake gave a soft chuckle. "You could be right, think I'll chance it. I'll give them a day, then I'll go check them out."

Jake wandered into Bodie the following afternoon. He went to the general store where he figured he could pick up some information. He opened the door and froze, there at the counter stood Vic and One Eye. He made a dash for the lady's department, hoping they would not spot him there. Only from here he could not hear what was being said.

Vic soon left and Jake mosied up to the counter and asked, "Say, what were those fellows after?"

"They were askin' questions about the group of people that were bothering the Chinese slaves the day he was here. Said he

141

left something with one of them and can't remember which one it was. I told them the only one I knew anything about that was with them the most was the singin' feller. Then the big feller says, 'Yeah, that's the one.' And then he asks me where he lives and, of course, I can't tell him 'cause I don't know. But I'm sure someone in town knows where that singer lives. Do you?"

Jake didn't answer, he was already on his way out the door.

After Jake left, Cad and Lin Chu decided to walk down to Pete's place. Upon seeing the two, Pete exploded, "Cad, you stupid son-of-a-bitch, air ya tryin' ta get yerself killed? Jake told ya ta stay home and here ya air, wanderin' around. Those ornery fellers could be right around here and that Chinese boy is a dead giveaway. I don't understand how a grown man can be so dumb."

Cad just stood and looked at him. It never occurred to him that this could be so. He and Lin Chu hung around Pete's most of the afternoon. Finally Pete could take it no longer. "Cad, Gawd damn it, go home. I cain't take the risk with my family by havin' ya hang around here no more. Yer makin' me jumpy as a cat."

Cad hung his head. Hell, couldn't he do anything right? Of course, he was placing the whole family in danger by staying here. He took Lin Chu and struck out for home, but instead of sticking to the road or the dry wash, he took off uphill to circle around in back. This was also a foolish move as it was the long way around and completely out of sight of Pete or any other help.

His lungs had been bothering him again lately and the long hard climb up the steep rocky slope started him coughing. By the time he crested the hill and started toward the shack, his lungs felt like they were bursting and spots formed before his eyes, pain shot through his chest, lights flashed in his head and giving one huge rasping cough, blood spewing from his mouth, he dropped to the ground.

Lin Chu was terrified. He fell to his knees calling, "Misee Cad! Misee Cad! You say something to Lin Chu. Lin Chu frightened. Please, Misee Cad!" Lin Chu did not hear the three men until they were directly on top of him.

"Wal, now, Bill, lookee here what we found."

"Looks like yer search is over, Vic, only it looks like yer too late to teach that singin' feller a lesson. He's already dead. Gawd damn, look at the blood all over his face."

Vic stared at Cad. It was one thing to kill a man, but to see this was kinda spooky. He reached down and grabbed Lin Chu by the queue and tied his hands behind his back. "Now, I'm gonna show you what they do with runaway slaves." He wrapped the end of the rope around the horn of his saddle and spurring his horse, raced off down the hillside dragging Lin Chu behind him through the rocks. By the time they reached the road, Lin Chu was dead.

Vic reached behind him, cut the rope, and the three men rode off down the road out of town.

Jake hurried up the path to the shack. He burst through the door calling, "Cad? Cad? Where the hell are you?" He pulled back the hanging to the mine entrance and called, "Cad?" It was dark down there, no Cad would not be down there. He walked up to the top of the hill and cupping his mouth with both hands called, "Cad, Lin Chu?" Nothing. The only other place he could be would be Pete's. He would have to hurry as it was beginning to get dark.

As he came down off the path on to the road, he saw a dark form lying, perhaps a yard or so up the road. Fear ran cold fingers down his spine as he headed for it. It was Lin Chu, my God, what a cruel and inhumane thing to do to the boy.

Pete saw Jake coming and with sudden fear, went to meet him.

"Pete?" Jake asked, "You seen Cad? I found the Chinaman's

body back down there in the road but I cannot find Cad."

"Oh God," said Pete, "wait a minute, I'll get my gun and a lantern and we'll go lookin'. He left here this afternoon and I thought sure he'd go straight home." He went for his gun while Jake tried to think what Cad would do and where he would go.

Pete returned saying, "He went off this way, Jake, let's see if I kin pick up his trail." They found where Lin Chu had been dragged out onto the road and followed the bloody trail back up the hill. They came to where Cad lay, still alive but in sad shape.

"Looks like Cad had another lunger, bad one this time. They must have thought he was already dead or they would have killed him for sure."

They pulled Cad to his feet and worked to arouse him. He finally moaned, and with an arm around both of his friends, staggered on to the shack. It took both Jake and Pete to clean him up, put him to bed and dress him in sheep fat and herbs. Cad, barely conscious, realized he was encased in the infamous sheep fat remedy again. *Shit!* he thought as darkness surrounded him again.

The long days crept by but Cad never did fully recover. It was quite evident that he was failing after a week of the healing oils that were doing Cad no more good. After that, Cad spent many of his days sitting on a large boulder on top of the hill behind the shack.

On one of Jake's trips to town, he heard of the fate of Vic and his men. Apparently after working Cad and Lin Chu over, Vic and his men were attacked by some of the escaped Chinese who cut off their own queues, tied them around the necks of the three, and throwing their bodies over their horses sent them back to Bodie. *Well*, thought Jake, *all's even again.*

He stopped by Pete's place on the way home only to find Pete's missus was down with the same kind of fever as his daughter, Clara. It almost acted like Cad's consumption in its early stages. He hoped it wasn't for he did not like to see someone die a slow death. It was evident that Pete was not leaving Bodie this year and the two men decided to take the wagon and head for the sawmill to gather winter fuel. The wood Jake had bought when he was ambushed had nearly been used by Pete in his smelting operation. Now it was time for more. Fall was upon them and the winds blew with a mighty fury, sometimes furnace hot, other times with a chill in the air. Pete and Jake talked of Cad, they both knew he would never make it through the winter. Cad's continual self-blaming for the fate of the Chinese people and the Potter family kept his health upset. Pete was also worried about his women folk.

"I jest gotta get outta this country, Jake boy, before I lose my family." Jake agreed.

A few days later they took the wagon down the road to the sawmill and brought home a large load of wood. Then the next day, another load and still another. Sick folk need to be kept warm. They packed and stacked and finally were ready to go into Bodie to pick up winter supplies of food.

Pete went back to smelting and Jake went back to working his mine.

The hole in the hill was getting deeper and longer. It was becoming increasingly harder to pack the ore up and out of the mine. Cad was absolutely no help with the mine but did work around the shack.

As the weather grew colder, Cad grew weaker. Most of his days were spent bundled warmly and sitting on the hearth before the fire. A certain amount of coldness seemed to creep up out of the mine and chill him to the bone although Jake tried to close it off as best he could, and finally ended up closing the mine up for a while.

The rainy season was well upon them when Cad caught a cold that turned into pneumonia. From there, he grew progressively worse. Pete never came to visit anymore because, though his wife was now well, his daughter, Clara, was getting weaker and weaker.

One morning Jake awoke to a blinding snowstorm. There didn't seem to be any way to get the shack warm. Cad was beginning to cough up blood and Jake held him in his arms to keep him from choking on it. He held him in his arms all that day and sometime in the early hours of the next morning, Cad doubled up in a spasm, gave several rasping coughs, blood spewing all over him, and died in Jake's arms.

CHAPTER TWENTY-THREE

IT WAS a long, lonely, cold winter for Jake. He had loved Cad like a brother and in his memory, Cad's beautiful singing voice filled the air. He could hear it in the wind and in the silence of his room. It floated through the corridors of his mind until the sadness within him was pure pain. He knew he had to get out and get busy. Pete was having his own problems. His daughter, Clara, was near death and sadness was thick in their shack also. They would only add to each other's pain, so Jake stayed away.

The need to be around people drove Jake to Bodie. He and Blaze trudged through the snow into town. The larger placer mine above town was in full swing and the town seemed overflowing with men. It amazed Jake that there was anyone left in town. There was at least one killing every day and as many disappearances. It seemed it was a stopping off place for every thief, bandit or highwayman in the country. The townspeople periodically appointed themselves as guards on the stages or freight wagons that carried gold out of Bodie. The gold would disappear anyway, so would the erstwhile upstanding citizens. Though there was never any proof, it looked mighty suspicious and it got to the point you didn't trust anyone anymore.

One of Jake's new friends was Lola whom he met at the Nugget Saloon one night when he was about half drunk. Jake was drinking a lot these days. He sat at a table in the corner where he could watch the activity around him, suddenly she was sitting beside him. She was a heavyset girl with eyes and hair as black as night. Her skin was milky white and much of it was showing. Jake looked at her through foggy eyes and soggy mind. *Now what the hell does she want?* he wondered, as she smiled and spoke. "Do ya mind? I'm bushed and need to rest a spell."

Jake shook his head. "No, no, he didn't mind." She sat and fanned herself staring shamelessly at Jake.

"Say, how come yer drownin' yer sorrows? You feelin' sorry fer yerself? Or do ya got troubles?"

Jake looked at her through bleary eyes and said, "Losht my best friend and I'm washin' out my sadness."

"Well, that will do it fer awhile but yer sure gonna feel like hell tomorrow." Her eyes twinkled as she smiled at him, "By the by, my name's Lola, what's yers?"

"Jake (hic) Jake Stone, (burp) and I think itsh time fer me to go home (hic)."

Jake struggled to his feet and held onto the table for support. The room was reeling dizzily and he was afraid to let go. Lola came around the table and took hold of his arm. "Better let me help ya there, Jake, ya don't look too steady to me."

Jake put his arm heavily around Lola's neck and whispered, "I brought my...my (hic) mule an if'n ya can jest point me at him (burp), he'll do the resht."

Lola managed to find Blaze and get Jake aboard. As Blaze headed out of town, Lola called, "Come on back tomorrow, Jake, okay?"

Jake reeled along on Blaze's back for a short while, then suddenly leaned over and was violently sick. How he made it back to the shack he didn't know but he sure was grateful to Blaze. He plopped down on his bunk, grabbed the sides and rode out the bucking and wheeling motions of the room.

Around afternoon the next day he awoke to a throbbing, pouncing head. "Oh, Gawd, I ain't cut out to be the town drunkard. He staggered to his feet, took the wash pan and put some cold water in it. He then went outside and poured it over his head. "Pfooy!" The mules were standing by the stable door looking at Jake. "I suppose you all got something to say about this? Like when are you going to feed me? And you, Blaze, you poor devil, still all saddled up from last night. Well, come here, old friend, let's get that stuff off of you and feed the rest of the gang."

The fire had gone out during his stay in town and he walked down to the ditch where he and Pete had stacked the firewood. The day was crisp and clear with a hint of spring to it. The mules munched grain as he fixed himself a light meal washed down with a gallon of black coffee. While he ate, he thought of Pete and realized it had been some time since he had seen the Dunning family and wondered how Clara was doing. He decided to put a large log on the fire and go down to see them. He found them in deep mourning. Clara had died during the night. He joined them in their sorrow and together they mourned their losses.

Winter was fickle this year. Blowing bitter cold one minute and hot the next. The wind blew the snow, piling it high against the walls of the hut and against the bank in back of it. Then along would come the warm winds, rapidly melting the snow, creating floods and causing all kinds of damage. There was so much water that Jake's mine was totally full and on the verge of welling up out into the room. He was constantly shoveling mud out the front door and the gap that occurred from the hill in back washing out, let in the cold winds. Then suddenly the winds would change and warm weather would set in and he would try to repair his roof and extend the hut.

It was almost two weeks since Jake was last in Bodie and since he needed more materials, he saddled Blaze and took off for town. His first stop was the lumberyard in back of the large Placer Mine. Lumber and firewood were higher than the price of gold per ounce this time of year. He found two large beams, paid the man telling him he would pick them up last. He then headed for the general store.

As he entered the store, he met Lola coming out. She stopped, greeting him warmly. "Wal, hello there, Jake, how come it took you so long to come back?"

Jake's mouth fell open and he stared at her. He could not for the life of him remember her but she sure seemed to know him. He felt embarrassment creeping over him. She laughed a hearty laugh saying, "Say, boy, I believe you were drunker than I knew. Don't ya remember nothing? I put ya on that white-faced mule of yours and sent ya home. Lola's the name."

Jake felt miserably embarrassed and wondered how he could have forgotten someone like her. "I'm afraid you're right, Miss Lola, I sure was dead drunk 'cause I sure don't remember you. And I'd have to be plum outta my head to forget someone as lovely as yourself."

"Hey, that's a pretty flowery speech there, Jake. Why don't cha come on over to the saloon and have a drink? We can set down and talk a spell." Jake assured her he'd do just that as soon as he finished his business at the store.

Jake took some time picking out the things he needed. He packed them carefully and tied them on Blaze. Taking Blaze by the bridle he walked up to the Nugget Saloon.

He walked inside and spotted Lola in the far corner. She waved and motioned for him to join her. Taking off his hat and wiping his mouth on the back of his hand in embarrassment, he strode over to where she sat.

"You know, Jake, I figured you to be standing me up again."

"Well, no, ma'am, I said I'd be here, and here I am." He grinned sheepishly.

She laughed at him and asked, "What are ya gonna have to drink, Jake? I'll bring it to ya since I'm startin' work in about five minutes."

"Just bring me a whiskey," he said, eyeing her as she took off her coat. She disappeared behind a door where she obviously left her coat and emerged ready for work. She wore a long black dress ornamented with red and black feathers and sequins. With her black hair and eyes and that milky white skin, she was stunning. Being a lot of woman in the right places, there was a lot of Lola showing out the top of her gown. Seeing her thus made Jake nervous and he was hard put to keep his eyes where they belonged. *I wonder what is behind her interest in me,* Jake thought.

Several men stopped Lola as she went to order Jake's drink. She picked up the whiskey and reached for a black book hanging on a peg behind the bar end. Jake wondered if she was making bookings for herself. He was sure she was a prostitute. She had to be to work in a place like this. The men disappeared out the back door as Lola brought Jake his drink. Well, he'd just drink his whiskey and be on his way.

Lola stood and made small talk with Jake for a while but business was heavy and she soon left Jake, becoming involved with the customers. As he watched her, Jake noticed that she reached often for the big black book but she never left the saloon. The other girls checked the book often and left by the mysterious back door, but Lola never did. Jake sat back and watched her. It was now obvious she was the house booker for the other prostitutes. He kinda wondered if she had ever been one of the girls or only the booker. *Why was she involved in this kind of dirty business? And, had she always been?* She wandered over for a minute and placed a hand on Jake's shoulder.

"Can I get ya another drink, Jake?"

"No, thank you, Miss Lola. I gotta be getting."

He arose from the table and tipping his hat, he hunched his way through the crowd to the door. *Damn*, groaned Jake, *this crooked body of mine is giving me fits again.* Grabbing Blaze's bridle, he led the mule down to the lumberyard. There the men helped him hitch the beams to a makeshift wimple tree and Jake headed home.

By the time he reached the shack he could hardly move his sore body around. He unhitched Blaze, unsaddled him, deciding to turn in for the rest of the day. He stoked the fire and after putting on the makings of a good old-fashioned stew, he pulled his bunk over by the fire where he stretched out, closing his eyes. God, how his body hurt.

CHAPTER TWENTY-FOUR

THE FOLLOWING DAY he resumed work on the hut. He struggled and mortared and beamed and thatched until he could hardly move. It was just about dark and the pain in his back was almost unbearable. He hunched into the hut and dished up a bowl of stew. Having hunted in vain through everything for a bottle of whiskey to help deaden the pain, he ate his soup and decided to go into Bodie where he could at least sit in a warm saloon and keep his mind off his pain by watching the people. He must be picking up a touch of rheumatism in this crooked old back, he thought.

Tying Blaze in front of the Nugget Saloon, he went in. The place was crowded and filled with smoke, the smell of whiskey filled the air with its sour smell and laughter rode around the room like a happy spirit. He spotted his favorite corner table and ambled over to it. Before he could be seated, Lola was at his side. What could this confounded woman want with him anyway?

"Evenin', Jake, what's yer pleasure?"

"Just bring me a bottle of whiskey, Lola, and let me sit."

"What's the matter, fella? Ya don't look so good."

"Just bring me the whiskey and never mind how I look." He waved his arm in the direction of the bar. She shrugged her shoulders and went for the bottle. Jake shifted uncomfortably in the chair. God, how he hurt!

Lola came back with the bottle. She eyed Jake as he shifted. Jake downed two or three fast shots, feeling the warmth filling his stomach, spreading along his limbs. It helped ease the pain all right, but not enough.

Finally, Lola came over and sat down. "Really hurtin', ain't ya, Jake?" He nodded. "I got somethin' in my room that will help, if ya want ta come with me. But ya ain't to get any ideas about sleepin' with me, ya understand?"

Jake nodded again. He could hardly get up from the chair, he was so stiff and sore. She led him through the crowded room to a narrow hall. At the end was a door that opened into a large room filled mostly with a large bed with many cloth trappings around it. It was all red, white and gold and smelled strong of cheap perfume. She motioned him toward the bed saying, "Take off your shirt, Jake, and let me rub some liniment on yer back."

"No!" shouted Jake. He stood, fear showing in his face. No woman had ever seen his crooked back and he was not about to let this stranger do so.

"Aw, come on, Jake. I been nursin' sick people all of my life and I see bodies worse than yers. I can help ya get comfortable and ease the pain in yer whole body."

Jake stood shaking and still refused to undress. She poured him a glass of water and handed both to him. "Here, take this, you can't imagine how good it can make ya feel. It's called 'morphine.'"

He took the pill and sat back down on the bed. Lola made small talk and he listened silently as he glanced around the room. It seemed to him that she had some pretty expensive furnishings here. It wasn't long before the pill began to take effect and the pain began to slowly fade away.

"Now, Jake, before ya get any more relaxed, take off yer shirt." Jake slowly began to unbutton his shirt. From a fuzzy distance he could feel her helping him. She rolled him over on his stomach and he could feel the soothing heat of the liniment and softness of her hands as he drifted off to sleep.

After making sure he was really out, Lola started going through his clothes. She turned his pockets inside out, testing seams for hidden pockets that might have been sewn into the cloth, looking for signs of maps or drawings that might indicate he had a gold mine or hidden gold somewhere.

Damn, thought Lola, all he's got is about twenty dollars in silver.

About that time there was a knock at the door. "Come on in," Lola called.

The door opened and a small, impeccably dressed man came through the doorway. He glanced around the room as he took off his white gloves. He was dressed all in gray, perfectly groomed in every way. His eyes rested on Jake. "Well, my dear, what have you found?"

"Mr. Lord, there ain't nothin' on the old codger."

"Please, my dear, don't use the word ain't or vulgar language." He lowered his brows. "You must act the part of a lady. Please, get away from the man and let me have a look at him."

He walked over to where Jake lay sprawled out on the bed. He took his cane and poked through Jake's clothing, touching nothing with his hands. "Yes, this is the gentleman I was talking about. Now, there must be something hidden somewhere on the man's person. I do know for a fact that he and two of his partners were working on a very high-grade ore mine. I also know he lost the mine and his partners were killed.

155

And, my dear, he deposited a great amount of money in the bank in Carson City. Now, it has to come from somewhere. My God, but he has an ugly looking spine."

He poked at Jake with his cane. "Keep at him, Lola, and when you find something out, send a man to Carson City and I'll return with him."

He put his gloves back on, picked up his hat, and spoke. "If you would be so kind as to open the door for me, my dear, I do not want to touch anything." He disappeared through the door wiping off his hat with a sparkling clean handkerchief, turned, handed the handkerchief to Lola, saying, "Please dispose of this dirty thing for me, will you? And I expect to hear from you real soon."

Lola closed the door and leaned against it. "That sterilized bastard," she spoke aloud. "Sterilized clean outside but puss rotten inside." She stood looking at Jake and a wave of remorse swept through her body. What was she trying to do to this poor unfortunate man? Hadn't life dealt him enough rotten blows with that awful back without them bastards trying to take the rest of his life too? She walked over and covered Jake with a quilt and went back out to work.

Jake stirred as she closed the door. His mind had recorded most of the conversation between Lola and Mr. Lord. He had not seen the man for his head was turned, but he knew that name and that voice. The man seemed to plague him. It seemed that he was behind most of the crime in Bodie. He also heard Lola as she expressed her distaste for the man. Wonder how she became mixed up with a man like him? He tried to move but his head was still buzzing and he still felt groggy. He noticed the pain in his back was gone and he was warm and comfortable under Lola's quilt. He was dozing again when Lola came back.

She went over and touched him on the shoulder. "Say, Jake, are ya gonna stay out forever?"

Jake rolled over and sat up. Boy, how his head went round and round. Lola was standing in front of him holding a pot of coffee and a mug. "Here," she said, "put some of this under yer belt. It'll help take away some of the buzzin'."

Jake sat holding the mug with both hands and wondered if he should tell her now that he had heard most of the conversation or wait and let her play her hand out. He decided that, at least for tonight, he'd drop it. All he wanted now was to go home.

He stood up, put on his shirt and coat. Then looking Lola straight in the eye, said, "I must go home now, I thank you for whatever it was that took away the pain. And that's all I'm gonna say to you right now."

He was still feeling a little dizzy as he made his way through the saloon and out to where he had tied Blaze. The mule raised his head and squeaked a small rusty bray at him. A light snow was falling again and Blaze was covered with it. Jake swept the snow from the saddle, then mounting, headed for home.

CHAPTER TWENTY-FIVE

BY MORNING, THE snow was almost gone. There was a bright morning sun, puffs of clouds all around. It was late January but the day hinted of an early spring. Jake set about finishing the repairs to his shack and wondering how much longer he was going to be able to hide the mine. With people like Lola and the Lord gangs around, no man and his gold were safe. And speaking of Mr. Lord, he had the feeling he was not through with him yet. He stood for a minute looking off toward Pete's place. He could see smoke curling through the air. *I wonder what my old friend is doing these days*, Jake thought. Since the water still was not gone from the shaft, and so much mud had washed into it, it was not possible to work the mine yet. So he guessed he would wander on down and check on the Dunnings.

Pete was making repairs on his two covered wagons. His wife, Alice, was sewing new canvas for the tops. They had been in Bodie for four years and much replacement and repairs had to be made in preparation for their leaving.

"Gol dang it, Pete," Jake said, "when the hell are ya leavin'?"

"Wal, not till spring, Jake, but I feel spring will be early this year and we're gonna have ta hurry along." Pete's two youngest boys, Alex, fourteen, and Joe, sixteen, were busy working over the harness.

"Pete, are ya gonna try to take all that gold back to Texas?"

"Yep."

"But, gosh darn it, man, that ain't safe."

"It's as safe as you all agoin' ta Carson City the way ya did."

"No, it ain't. You're going a lot farther and taking a bigger risk. It'd be worth your while to take 'er into Carson City and sell it. Then have a bank draft sent to a bank in Texas."

"No, sir. I ain't trustin' no mail to carry my money. And that piece of paper ain't worth nothin'.'"

"Pete, how can a man with as much horse sense as you be so stubbornly stupid about this? You helped me, but when it comes to your own money, you can't seem to think straight."

"No, sir, Jake, yer all wrong. I ain't goin' through the same country and no one would think I'd be carrin' gold all the way to Texas. And besides, I intend to fill the bottom of that false bottom wagon ya brought back. Plus, I'll get enough mules to pack the rest. Got it all figured out, Jake, man."

"No, Jake, yer all wrong this time, boy."

Jake threw up his hands in hopelessness. He could see there wasn't much he could do or say that would change Pete's mind.

Pete Dunning was a quiet man. He made no fuss over the gold claim he had found. He worked quietly and doggedly. The claim was a small one and his efforts chipping the ore only made a good haul for outlaws. He then put all his efforts into smelting it into small bars. The outlaws made a couple of raids and cleaned him out. He then moved to this spot, which was only a little better than the last one, but Pete had learned how to hide the little gold bars so no one could find them and raids finally broke off. Illness had plagued the family the last few years. He had lost two of his daughters and now his wife, Alice, was in a fetish to get the rest of the family out of this Godforsaken country. Pete had pretty well worked out his claim and there was nothing now to hold him in Bodie.

Jake worked with them for well over a week and a half. Then came the day of departure. Jake awoke early that morning. He walked outside and surveyed the country. His eyes came to rest on the hill back of Pete's. Hmmm! Two horsemen. How what in the hell were they watching? He stood there and watched. The men dismounted and backed their horses out of sight, then placed themselves amongst the rocks as if to wait.

Jake did not stop to fix breakfast. He worked his way through the rocks and headed north until he was sure he was out of sight. Then worked his way down to Pete's place and told him what he had seen.

"I've got a feelin', Pete, that they're just awaitin' fer you to pull out."

Pete rubbed his hand across his chin and walked back and forth. He called to his wife, "Alice, you all come here and listen."

His wife came over to where he was. He reached out and took her by the arm. "Turn around and keep your backs to the hill. We've got company up thar and this will confuse them, make them think we don't know they're thar. We cain't pull up stakes right now, if'n we do, we could all be killed. Now, girl, you walk in and fix us something to eat, jest like it was any other day. Jake and I air gonna do some figurin'."

The two men walked over to the smelting pot. "Jake, I'm gonna leave this monstrosity to you. Thar ain't no more ore in that diggin' of mine, but the boys have been pretendin' thar is. They been loadin' up a few bags of rock. Now, if'n you all got any ore ya want broken down, jest lug it on down after dark. That'll give me somethin' to work on. Make them think I'm not goin anywhere. 'Course, the wagons are almost packed and they may have seen that, then again, maybe they haven't."

"That sounds pretty good, Pete. I do have about ten bags of ore swimmin' around in that gol dang hole. This all makes me worried about getting my own gold outta Bodie. That Mr. Lord was in Bodie a week or so ago. I had another little incident again. I have a feeling he's behind a lot of the problems that the Bodie miners have."

"What do ya mean? Did ya have another run in with that walkin' bar of soap."

"No, not a run in, just an incident." Jake did not want to tell Pete about Lola and his bout with the morphine. He felt more than a little stupid for letting that woman get to him. "I think I'll make good use of my time working on another plan to get my gold out of Bodie. Maybe this time, for good."

The two men stood looking at the pots. Pete bent down and placed some wood under the pots and began stoking up the fire.

Alex and Joe came running out. "Hey, Pa, whatcha doin', I thought we were leavin'?"

Pete took the boys aside and explained it to them, giving them instructions as to what they were to do. "We're bein' watched and you boys are to act and do jest like any other day. Understand? Keep your eyes at home, don't keep lookin' around at the road or hills or anythin'."

"Oh boy, we got us a gen-u-ine adventure," Alex said gleefully.

Jake said farewell and headed back the way he had come. He fixed his breakfast, fed the mules, and set to cleaning out the trench through the house so the water could flow freely from the mine. Then taking a bucket, he walked into the mine and for the rest of the day he baled water. He then carried the bags of ore out and put them in the mules' stall. Occasionally he would look out the door to see if the men were still over on the hill. They were pretty well covered and only by careful scrutiny could he detect any movement.

As night fell, Jake placed the bags of ore on top of the mules and went down to Pete's where he unloaded it in the smelting shed. The night was so dark he could hardly see two feet in front of his face. He was glad the mules could find their way home. He stood outside the hut staring over at the hill. Either the men had gone or they were not lighting any fires.

The following morning he was up before down. He walked outside and sat on a rock watching the hill and waited. When there was just enough light to see by, he noticed movement. It looked like two riders coming from the direction of Bodie. Ah ha! He figured they would leave for the night and come back for the day. Suddenly he saw more horsemen who rode over to meet the others. They then headed back for Bodie. Well now, that's a different story. Maybe he should wander into Bodie also. He could look up Lola and have a drink with her. Maybe she and Mr. Lord are behind this too. After all, they were after news of his gold and maybe his friendship with Pete made them put two and two together.

He saddled Blaze and turned toward Bodie. As he rounded the bend a gang of horsemen came riding down the road. They did not look like miners and seemed to be in a big hurry. Jake hunched over and pulled to one side to allow them to ride through.

Fear churned in Jake's stomach. He wondered if they were headed for Pete's place. He turned Blaze up a small hill to see if he could spot Pete's shack but the hill was not high enough. He followed the cloud of dust with his eyes. It appeared as though they were headed on down the road. Jake sighed with relief and continued on to Bodie.

He pulled up in front of the saloon, went in and looked around the dim room for Lola. She was nowhere in sight. He went to the bar and ordered himself a drink. Taking his drink with him, he wandered around from game to game listening to different conversations but could not pick up any information.

He found a table over by the roulette game and sat down. The wheel was busy and various groups of men came and went around it. He heard one story that interested him and he placed the young man in his mind for further conversation, then boldly walked down the hall and knocked on Lola's door. There was no answer so he knocked again, still no answer. He tried the door. Open! Glancing back over his shoulder to see if anyone were watching him, he walked in. Softly he closed the door, turned and gasped in horror! Lola lay across her bed, blood covered her face and great welts and bruises covered her arms and shoulders. Jake went over to her and raised her head. She was still alive but unconscious. He did not know what to do. Noticing there were no locks on the door and fearing someone would come in and blame him for the deed, he pushed the dresser over in front of it.

Finding a pitcher of water, some towels and salve, he went to Lola and stood over her. He was going to have to remove her blood-soaked clothing and change the sheets. The sheets were easy but the clothes were something else again. Never having viewed a woman's naked body, sweat was beginning to form on his upper lip. Well, if he were to help her at all, he was going to have to get busy.

Jake began by washing her face. There seemed to be several cuts that were bleeding profusely, also a large gash across the back of the head. He gingerly took off her outer clothes, left her in her chemise, and wrapped her in a blanket. She was a large girl and he knew he could not lift her, so he rolled her gently from side to side of the bed to the other to change the bedding. He had some trouble locating the things he needed and by the time he had finished, she was coming to. "Oh, my God, I ache."

"Now, Miss Lola, you must lie quiet while I finish cleaning you up. Do you suppose you could tell me where I might find bandages?"

She rolled her head back and forth causing the scalp wound to start bleeding again. "Now, Lola, hold your head still. There is a gash that keeps bleedin' and I just changed your sheets. Just tell me where the stuff is and I'll bandage you all up."

She pointed to a cabinet above the table. "There's all the necessary stuff."

Jake stood back and looked at her. She looked more like a poorly wrapped mummy than a well-bandaged victim. Oh well, at least she wasn't bleedin' all over the place. He helped her into a sitting position.

"There now, tell me what happened."

Lola stared at him. "What are ya doin' here anyway, Jake Stone?"

"I wanted to talk to you, ask a few questions. I didn't see you in the saloon so I came back and knocked on your door. There wasn't any answer so I tried the handle and, sure enough, it opened. Then I saw you. You were all full of blood and badly bruised. I was afraid someone would come back and think I did it, so I blocked the doorway with your dresser."

Lola put her hands to her head and pushed the bandage out of her eyes. "Yeah, but what were ya lookin' fer?"

"You."

"Okay, so now ya found me. But yer bein' here just puts me back in the middle of trouble."

"Why?"

"Oh, Jake, cain't ya just take my word fer it and go away and leave me alone? Please? All I kin tell ya is, yer my trouble."

Jake looked long at her. "I know that, Lola, but I want you to tell me why."

Lola burst into tears. "I cain't, Jake, I jest cain't," she sobbed.

"You might just as well because I already know. You see, your magic medicine didn't quite knock me out and I heard most of your talk with Mr. Lord."

Lola gasped, "Oh God, no."

"Now, why don't you tell me how you find out all your information? Do you dope all your customers? Did you get some information on my friend, Pete? Come on, girl, talk." Jake shook her by the shoulders but she just lay there sobbing.

"I couldn't find nothing on you, Jake, and Mr. Lord wouldn't take no for an answer. There's a young miner who's been sneaking over to the Dunnings' to see Jessie, the older girl. He's the one I got the information from on yer friend, Pete."

Jake arose and stood looking at the girl. He was seething inside. She looked so pitiful but he couldn't feel sympathy for her right now.

"How could you stoop so low, Lola? How could you? What in hell's name would make a woman like yourself do such lousy, lowdown things to a man?"

Lola turned over on her face and sobbed into her pillow. Jake turned on his heel and unbarring the door, left.

He went on out into the saloon and looked around for the young miner he had overheard at the wheel. Jake was sure he was the young man Lola was talking about, but he was nowhere in sight. He took off, making the rounds of the rest of the drinking holes but he was nowhere to be found. He had forgotten to ask Lola the young man's name and he did not feel like going back and taking a chance of being found there in her room. It was turning dark now so Jake crossed the street to the café for some supper. He just didn't feel like going home and fixing it.

It was late by the time Jake reached home and he fell into his bunk, sleeping hard and long.

The sun was high in the sky by the time Jake awoke. He made a fire and fixed himself some breakfast, then wandered outside to feed the mules. He walked around to a spot where he could see the hill back of Pete's. There was no movement. He parked himself on a rock to watch. *Hmmm! Nothing, I wonder if they've given up?*

CHAPTER TWENTY-SIX

HE STARTED DOWN the hill and headed off to Pete's. As he rounded the bend he stopped in horror. Gone! Everyone was gone! "Oh, my God." Jake spoke aloud. He didn't know what to do. He was sure there would be foul play. There was so much indication of it. He walked on into the deserted camp, the old lean-to and hut looked decrepit and empty, as if no one had lived there for years. Jake wandered through everything. As he came out to the old smelting pot he noticed a paper nailed to the frame. Plucking it off, he read:

Jake, old pard. Had to leave before ya tried ta talk me outta it. I don't believe the danger is as bad as ya make it out ta be. There are many more richer miners to be had than myself. I think you outta get out of Bodie yerself before you cain't. God shoulda made more men like yerself, Jake, and I give you his blessings. If ya ever get to Texas, be sure ta

look us up. We all think the world of ya, Jake.
Take care of yerself.
    Yer old pard, Pete.

Jake took a deep breath. Well, they were sure on their way, all right. He hoped they would make it. He glanced over his shoulder to the top of the hill where the men had been watching. Maybe he'd just wander up that way. Upon reaching the top, he found the remains of a fire placed between large boulders. No wonder he couldn't see it at night, it was sure well hidden. He squatted down and placed his hands on the embers, still warm. That meant Pete had managed to pull out ahead of them. Maybe he had a real good start. Just maybe.

Looking off across the hills, Jake felt an engulfing wave of loneliness. His two closest friends were now gone. He heard a rusty bray from across the hills. Blaze had spotted Jake even at that distance. Jake felt the warmth of love for the only friend he had left. *That mule, he's almost human!* Standing up, he kicked the embers with his boot and headed for home.

Jake busied himself cleaning out his mine. The water had disappeared and the mud had dried out enough to haul out. He cleaned for several days until the mine was workable again. One day, in late afternoon, he decided to go over to Pete's and take old Blaze. Perhaps he could haul that old smelting pot over to his place. As he rounded the bend, he gasped, "What the hell?"

There stood two of Pete's mules with the remains of a wagon dragging behind them. Mud and sweat were caked to their bodies and blood had dried to their heels where the remains of the wagon banged against their heels while moving. Jake quickly unhitched the mules and they brayed gratefully. He cleaned them off and set them loose to graze. His heart was pounding and fear shook his body.

How many days had it been since Pete left? Four? Five? He

wasn't sure. He stood there in a state of shock trying to figure out what to do next. How long had the mules been back? It must have been for at least a day because they were dry and the bleeding at their heels had stopped.

Perhaps he should try to round up some of Pete's miner friends and hit the trail, see if they could find them. Well, standin' there wasn't going to get anything done, so move, feet. He took Blaze home and saddled him, then headed off up the hill toward Olsen's. The old miner was preparing to end the day's work. Jake hastily told him of what he had found and the two of them decided to search Bodie for men who would be willing to join them. They found four men and they made preparations for departure the following morning.

They met at Pete's old place at dawn the next morning and struck off for Mono Lake. At the bottom of the hill they stopped. Now which of the wagon trails did the Dunnings take? Trails led off in all different directions. They took the one that pointed toward Arizona and traveled all that day. Night found them without a suitable campsite. None of them had ever been that way and were not familiar with the territory. Grain had been packed and the animals had grain but none had water that night.

The following morning they came upon a stream, full flowing into a large pool. They made noon camp, fixing a small lunch and watering the animals. Jake made a survey of the area, walking around to the other side of the pool. Wagon tracks heading east toward Arizona, Jake counted three of them.

"Hey, men, over here," hollered Jake.

The men mounted and they rode in the direction of the wagon tracks.

About three hours later they came to a small uprising of ground. There they found the remains of what Jake knew to be Pete's body. There were signs of a scuffle but they could not find any more bodies. Rummaging through the debris, Jake was

169

able to identify Pete's belongings.

They dug a grave and buried what was left of Pete's body. As they were finishing someone called, "Hey, over here, look, wagon tracks, and they're heading south toward Texas. Let's go!"

"Wait a minute, young fella, where do you think you're goin'?"

"After them, after all, the man we buried might not be Pete. They may all be safely headed for home."

"No, that was Pete we buried all right, no mistake in that."

The young man slumped. "Well, I guess we'll never know if Jes—never know who all escaped. And if they ever made it home."

"Oh, I imagine someone will write and let us know."

"I can't help feeling coldhearted about the whole thing. Here we are, this far, and we give up and go home."

"Son, there is hundreds of heat racked miles out there. We do not have food or water or proper equipment of any kind for a journey out there. They could be days ahead of us. And what are you going to do when you do find them? Turn around and come back? If so, what good will you have done them? Unless you are prepared to go on to Texas with them, you're better off turning around now."

The young man stood staring off into the distance. "You know, Jake, I'm sick and tired of Bodie. Going to Texas doesn't sound that bad. I have a fast young horse, maybe I'll overtake them soon."

The men divided up their food and water with the young man who then mounted and took off at high speed. Jake stood watching him go. There goes the young fool after Jessie. He has no idea that he is undoubtedly the one to blame for the tragedy. Tears dimmed his eyes. He turned to the grave, took off his hat, knelt and prayed. The rest followed suit.

It was a long, silent trip back to Bodie. They followed the

stream part of the way. There was early spring grass and pools of clear water on the upper road to Bodie. Jake speculated on who escaped. Most likely all the women and the two boys would not have posed a threat to whoever had ambushed them. Pete had worked so hard and the family had put up with so much hardship that it was a pity. Jake pondered on the wickedness of the day, of Bodie and its evil ways. It seemed the gates of hell had opened up and all the evil therein settled in Bodie.

Hate began to burn in Jake's heart, hate such as he had never known. Somehow, he was going to beat that town and the infamous Mr. Lord who seemed to be a phantom in too many of the evil doings, both here and in Carson City. Well, by God, he was going to come out of that hellhole a winner. Those son-of-a-bitches were not going to get the best of him no more. No, sir! He would plan and work and they would play hell beatin' him.

The men began to talk amongst themselves but Jake rode in stony silence, planning his vengeance. Someone was gonna pay. By God, he'd find a way.

CHAPTER TWENTY-SEVEN

ALONG ABOUT THE first of May, Jake began to feel the need to see old friends. His vigilance on his lonely hill was getting to be almost more than he could bear.

He had not been to Bodie since he came back from burying Pete and he had only once seen one of the miners that had gone with him. No word had returned from the young man, Robert, and he wondered what had happened to the boy. He also wondered what had been happening in Carson City. He cautiously thought of Ruth and felt his pulse quicken. Ah, yes, he was still in love with that beautiful girl. There was a good deal of ore and dust that should be taken to Carson City. But then there was the mine and how would he keep it from being found. He could start by firing up Pete's old smelting pot and smelting as much of his ore as he could. Having inherited an old wagon from Pete, he began inspecting it for possibilities. As he stood gazing and rubbing his beard, an idea began to form. Yes, it could be done…maybe.

He hitched two mules to the wagon and headed for the

sawmill early the next morning. He loaded up with several long pieces of lumber, explaining to the talkative salesman that he needed a new bottom for his wagon as the other one was rotting out. By nightfall he was back home unloading the wagon and feeding himself and the mules. After supper he sat down and by lantern light began to draw out his plan.

A frame of 2 x 4's, a bed of 1 x 4's nailed over it, all seams sealed with clay. Now, I'll take the rest of the 2 x 4's and split them thus [_____], nail them together, seal them with clay, and pour a layer of sheep fat into the bed. Wipe it off so the fat greases up the boards but does not take up room. Then pour the melted gold into the bed when it's cool enough not to melt the fat too much, and still hot enough to pour. That would give him a one-inch layer of gold in that wagon bed. Like this, he thought, as he drew out the plan.

2 x 4 whittled out gold layer

2 x 4 with   existing wagon
1 x 4 nailed to it   rotted bottom

All would be heavily nailed to the wagon bottom and sides.

Jake spent the rest of the month smelting and building his wagon. He also devised a covering for the mine entrance. He made a frame and covered it with burlap sacking. Then he plastered it with wet clay. He then allowed it to bake in the sun. When he was ready he would pull the frame inside, use more clay to seal the edges and hope no one would find it.

The day came when he was ready to place all the gold he had smelted into the pot and pour it into the wagon bottom. He had pulled one of Pete's old lean-to structures up to the hut and made a crude shelter over the wagon and smelting pot to keep them from sight. He spent three nights sleeping in the wagon with his shotgun across his lap. By the fourth morning his back was so stiff he could hardly get out of the wagon. With Blaze's help, he managed to move the smelting pot into the hut and into the mine entrance and to pull the heavy muddied frame into place. It was so heavy and awkward it wanted to fall into the room. He backed old Blaze up to the mud screen and made him sit. This held the frame in place until he could mud it to the hill. He then pulled the table and shelves over to brace the ends while he moved Blaze. Then, carefully shifting the shelves that held his supplies, he managed to place it dead center. Now no one could tell it was there except for the fresh mud. And it wouldn't be noticeable in a day or two.

He then packed a few things he needed, hitched four mules to the wagon and pulled off down the hill to Pete's old camp. There he picked and packed fifteen sacks of bad grade ore which were left in Pete's old mine and stacked them in the back of the wagon. *Good decoy*, thought Jake, *good decoy*.

He spent the early part of the night in Pete's old camp and just before dawn, pulled cautiously out into the road leading to Mono Lake. At the bottom of the hill he turned west and took the almost impassable trail for Carson City. It was a few minutes before sunrise by the time he hit the road north. The mules picked up speed once they were on the good road. About noon Jake spotted some riders a distance up the trail. He could not tell how many there were or if they were coming or going. He became nervous and kept glancing over his shoulder. He had placed wool pelts that Pete had left him over the sacks of gold ore, then tied it down with canvas. He hoped it all looked authentic.

Many hours later he came to the crossroads that led to Carson City.

Where were the riders? He had not seen any more signs of them. Perhaps they had been going the same way as he.

He turned the mules northwest and began looking for a place to camp. It must be a place with a good escape route. There was a ravine up ahead that he knew would be perfect. He pushed the mules in hopes of getting there before dark but the mules were tired and true to their nature, they were not going to be pushed. Not even the trustworthy Blaze could pull them along and it was well after dark when he reached the ravine. As he turned to go in, the two lead mules snorted and reared. There was a shot and then total blackness.

He came to with the awareness of pain in his head and shoulder. He put his hand to his head and felt the stickiness of blood. Blood was also coming from his shoulder. He was still lying in the seat of his wagon and it was moving along slowly. Sitting up, his head swimming, he tried to see in the darkness but could not get his bearings. He was alone and, obviously, the mules were just traveling by themselves.

"Whoa, Blaze, whoa, damn ya."

He grabbed for the reins but Blaze had already stopped by the time he found them. It was too dark to tell if he was traveling toward Carson City or Bodie. The land was flat with no place to hide. Turning the team off the road, he stopped. His head was throbbing and his shoulder was burning like hell. He turned slowly and climbed in the back of the wagon, not knowing if the sacks or the bottom of the wagon were still there. Cautiously he placed his feet on the back panel and groped for the bottom. Still there, by God! They also left him his sheep pelts and he threw himself down on them gratefully and fell asleep.

The sun was high when he awoke the next morning. His head still ached but his shoulder was numb. Examining his head and tracing the trail of blood, he found the crease where the bullet had grazed it. He gingerly lifted his shirt from his shoulder and saw the bullet had gone all the way through the fleshy part of his shoulder. Well, anyway he wasn't carrying any lead. Pulling out one of his shirts, he made a crude bandage and sling. *That's going to have to do*, Jake thought. He climbed

175

back into the wagon seat and picked up the reins. Glancing around at the lay of the land, he found that the mules had turned and headed back, as the crow flies, to Bodie. This road was not familiar to him but he recognized some of the distant landmarks. "Blaze, whoa boy, you're headed in the wrong direction. Let's get turned around and headed for Carson City while I can still make it." The bleeding had pretty well stopped but that might mean early infection. He had to get help.

The mules pulled out at a fair pace and as the wagon was several hundred pounds lighter, they could keep it up longer. Jake pushed on until they came to the main trail. He pulled up short. The mules had traveled a long way that night. He still had not reached the ravine where he had been ambushed. He pushed on until he came to the ravine. There he found most of his personal belongings strewn around the ground. The nosebags and grain were on the ground also. He climbed painfully down and after much labor, he had the nosebags on all the mules. The barrel of water he always carried had been tipped over and emptied. That meant a dry day until he could reach the roadside well. He still felt uneasy in that place while he and the mules rested. Keeping a sharp lookout for riders, he took off the nosebags and placed them along with the grain in the back of the wagon, turned the mules toward Carson City and moved out. It was night again, the stars were bright and there was a quarter moon to help light up the desert. He kept the team moving until he reached the roadside well.

He watered the mules and drank long himself, wishing now that he had not left the barrel back at the ravine. He could not have lifted the barrel anyway with this shoulder. Beginning to feel feverish, he washed his face in the cool water, wondering if it would be safe to camp for the rest of the night. There would be no more water until the following night from here, so he guessed he'd better chance it. Beginning to shiver, he crawled back onto the wagon and rolled himself up in a wool pelt, slept fitfully the remainder of the night. By dawn, he knew he'd better feed and water the mules and push on. The mules had to be fed by hand as the nosebags were too hard to handle.

He shivered uncontrollably. The fever was rising higher inside him. Crawling inside the wagon and wrapping himself in the sheep pelt, he headed on. As the day wore on, he felt fainter. The pain in his shoulder was a throbbing, searing pain. The mules were moving at a good steady trot and the miles crept by. As night drew on, they were still on the move and Jake could not think. He did not stop at the well. Left on their own, the mules kept their pace on toward Carson City. By morning, Blaze was in familiar territory and he picked up more speed. Jake had fallen over onto the floor, unconscious.

A day later Blaze led the team into the yard of the Garrett ranch. Ruth spotted the wagon and followed it down to the barn. When Jake came to, he was lying in a bed on clean white sheets and Ruth was sitting in a chair by the bed. *Well, I'm still alive*, thought Jake as he turned his head and fell asleep.

CHAPTER TWENTY-EIGHT

AT RUTH'S ORDERS, the ranch hands had carried Jake upstairs to the spare bedroom. Old Joe had undressed and cleaned him up, making ready for the two women to administer to his wounds. He shook his head as he came out of the door, "His shoulder looks real bad, Mrs. Garrett, real bad."

Both women gasped as they exposed the wound. It was swollen and angry looking with green fluid oozing from it. "Sarah, I'm going to send for the doctor," said Ruth as she ran from the room.

Once the wound had been lanced and cleaned, Jake healed rapidly. He also began worrying about the wagon. As soon as he gained enough strength, he went out to the barn to check on it, finding all in order. *That's a relief*, thought Jake. In a few days he would be strong enough to head for town.

Sarah and Ruth filled him in on what had been going on since he was here last. Jake had to admire the two women for the way they seemed to be managing the ranch and the boarding house. Sarah talked about selling off the back acreage, then

178

keeping the front acre with the house for room and board. She said she could keep the rooms filled most of the time. It was true, thought Jake, good honest foremen were hard to come by and a bad one could ruin you. Also, the town was beginning to creep their way.

Jake wondered about Ruth, if she had any admirers, or was she just keeping herself in here with her baby. Why hadn't she married yet? She kept following him around with adoring eyes, making him nervous, it also made him so very aware of the hump on his back. He tried many ways of escaping her but she always found him.

The day finally came when he felt well enough to hitch up the mules and head to town. The Wells Fargo Office greeted him warmly. It was always interesting when he came there for they never knew what trick he played this time to get his gold to town. They helped him tear down and unload his wagon while they laughingly told him how some poor miner had been robbed of his wagon full of gold ore only to find out the ore was all but worthless. Jake turned so he could watch them, they could not know they were talking about him. To Jake, it just confirmed his theory that the gang came out of Carson City and probably belonged to the Lord conglomerate.

Jake decided to risk a question. "Say, how well do you fellows know the man named Mr. Lord?"

One of the young men, a tall dark complexioned man, spoke. "Yeah, he owns the local funeral home down the street. A real overly clean, sickening sort of guy. Makes ya want ta go home and take a bath yerself after talkin' to him. Why?"

"I was just wondering."

"I hear say that he masterminds some rather shady deals," offered the other man, "and has something to do with several gangs of outlaws. Now, that is just hearsay, I really don't know anything myself for sure. I do know he hires some pretty tough characters that hang around him all the time."

Yeah, thought Jake, *I guess he does have some pretty tough characters around him. And I have a sneakin' hunch they were responsible for my ambush and I have a feeling he's out to make good his threat of 'sweet revenge.'*

He finished uncasing the gold, had it weighed out, banked part of it in an account for Ruth and kept the rest for himself. Now he felt Ruth would be adequately taken care of no matter what happened. It bothered him that she was not getting out and socializing.

They put the new planks back in the bottom of Jake's wagon and he headed for the general store. He needed some dynamite to open up his mine, that vein surely must go deeper than that. He purchased more clothing and staples, then moved on over to the doctor's office.

Looking across the street, Jake laughed to himself, *Lord's funeral parlor across from the doctor's office, mighty convenient.* He went into the office. There were two people ahead of him so he placed himself by the window where he could look out across the street.

The front of the funeral parlor appeared to have a new coat of gray paint, it looked as fresh and overly clean as the man himself. Even the boardwalk in front of the place was painted gray. As he watched, he noticed how the people would detour out in the street rather than walk on it. The whole place gave him the creeps. He wondered what excuse he could dream up that would take him inside of the place.

Suddenly the door opened and Mr. Lord emerged, dressed as usual, totally in gray. Behind him came two men dressed in black with white shirts and gloves. They paused, putting on their gloves, as if waiting for someone. Soon a buggy drove up, dark gray in color and pulled by the beautifully matched pair of dappled gray horses. The two men helped Mr. Lord into the buggy with a minimum amount of contact with the rigging, then taking the reins from the livery boy, they took their places on the front seat and all rode off down the street. Jake sat there shaking his head. Now, that was better than a sideshow.

He felt a hand on his shoulder and a voice saying, "It seems to me, Mr. Stone, your shoulder is better than your hearing. I've called you twice."

"Sorry, I was so busy watching the sideshow across the way, I didn't hear you call."

The doctor laughed, "Yeah, I can't make up my mind if he's alive or some half-dead stiff. I hear he's trying to court some girl out here on the edge of town somewhere. Can't imagine who would be able to stand a man like that. Understand, though, she's not too happy about the idea. Must be something else he's interested in, women aren't really his style."

The doctor dressed Jake's wound and told him he need not come see him again as the wound was healing well.

Jake stood on the sidewalk outside the doctor's office and wondered if the door was open across the street. Guess maybe he'd find out. When he got over there, he stopped just off the gray painted area. Hell, if he walked on the painted area the footprints would show someone walked in the door, and if he looked in the window, it would still show, and if he took off his boots, the whole gol-dang street would see him.

He heaved a sigh and went for his wagon. All the way to the ranch he tried to figure a way to catch that over-clean dude in a trap. He was so engrossed in his plan that when he turned into the lane, he did not see the gray buggy and team in the yard. Standing up in the wagon, he shouted, "Whoa, Blaze, back, back! Jesus, what the hell is he doing here?" He pulled hard on the reins and swung the wagon around and out the gate at a trot. He turned left and went down the road to a stand of trees where he hid out of sight. He tied the team to a branch and took a place on the ground where he could not be seen.

Being too far away from the ranch house to see clearly what was going on, he decided to work his way closer. There didn't seem to be anyone in the buggy and he guessed even the boys in black were in the house.

He walked up the irrigation ditch until he reached the gate, then crouched down to crawl up beside the house. He could barely hear the voices. He could distinguish Sarah's voice but could not hear Ruth's. A movement caught his eye. Turning quickly he saw the figure of Ruth running toward the bunkhouse. Jake followed her.

As he came around the corner, he startled her and she gasped, "Oh, Jake, Jake, am I glad to see you." She flung herself into his arms. "I couldn't stand that man another minute. He has been bothering me ever since the last time you were here. He keeps askin' questions about you, about Bodie, and about all your friends. I keep tellin' him I don't know anything about you or your friends."

"Well, it's a good thing you don't know anything about me. It's safer for you that way. Even Sarah doesn't know much about me. I would like you to do me a favor, Ruth. Go back in there with him, see if you can get any information from him on how much he knows about Bodie."

Ruth backed away and studied his face. "What do you mean, how much he knows about Bodie? Has something else happened, Jake?"

"Well, yes, Ruth, but I don't really want to burden you with ideas, thoughts and worries, so don't ask me no more, okay?"

Ruth nodded her head. "Yes, Jake, I'll do that for you." With that, she turned and walked back to the ranch house.

Jake stayed glued to the window of the bunkhouse. "Oh, my God, no! That gol dang mule," he said. Now, how the hell was he going to stop that? Blaze had broken loose and was coming up the road with the others and the empty wagon in tow. His ears were pointed forward and his head held high. "Oh, Jesus," Jake moaned. "He ain't gonna bray, is he? Hell, yes!" He put his hands over his ears as a rusty bray filled the air and Blaze pulled into the yard.

With no one to guide him, he pulled in wide at a good brisk trot. The wagon overshot, hit the back end of the buggy, which in turn, caused the gray team to be pulled off their feet, frightening them. As Blaze pulled around in front of them, he let out another hair-raising bray. The gray team scrambled to their feet pulling loose from the hitching post and tearing off out of the yard, turning toward town with the gray buggy bounding along like a leaf in the wind, to end up upside down in the irrigation ditch some three hundred yards away. The grays were rearing and pawing the air with their hooves but could not break away from the spinning wheels of the upside down buggy.

The back door opened and the two men in black plus a couple of ranch hands from the barn went running off down the road. Jake didn't know whether to laugh or cry. He couldn't see the front porch so he could not tell of Mr. Lord's reaction. He was sure that Mr. Lord was not aware he survived the ambush, let alone in town. He waited watching out the bunkhouse window and saw the ranch hand bring the team back with the two men in black running alongside dusting and wiping off the buggy as they ran.

Mr. Lord suddenly appeared, arms waving. Jake could hear shouting but could not understand what was being said. Not being able to help himself he slapped his hand against his knee and howled as the buggy headed off for town, the team at a gallop. Jake wondered if he had spoiled his plans, or rather if Blaze had. He walked out of the bunkhouse toward the barn. Blaze squealed and rubbed his head against Jake's chest. "Now, you love sick gol dang mule, how in hell can you be so stupid? How can I trust you to stay put when I ask you to? You ain't no help, and yet you're my best help. Everything you do always turns out right in the end." He patted, rubbed and loved the mule, all the while Blaze moaned and squeaked.

Unhitching the team and turning them loose in the corral, he walked up to the ranch house. Ruth came flying down the path with her head back laughing. He caught her up in his arms. "Jake, oh, Jake, did you see? Oh, how funny that big clown, Blaze. That was the most glorious thing I ever saw."

"I saw most of it, Ruth, but I could not see Mr. Lord till he left waving his arms and shouting. Come, let's go into the house and you can tell me about it." He opened the door for her and they joined Sarah in the kitchen who was still wiping her eyes and laughing.

Jake poured Ruth and himself a cup of coffee and sitting down at the table said, "Now, girl, suppose you tell me about it."

Both women began at once, then Ruth let Sarah take over. "First off, Jake, when Ruth saw the buggy turn into the yard, she took off for the bunkhouse. She's always leavin' me to wrangle with that bum. Wal, anyway, he starts in on what he could do for us if'n Ruth would jest marry him. How he would be a good father for little Sarah and how good he would be to Ruth. He's always dustin' off a place to sit down and linin' it with his clean white hanky so my dirty furniture won't stain his milky white bottom. Always a'makin' me feel so dirty I cain't stand ta see him come. He always makes Ruth wash her hands in some stuff he carries around in a little white bottle so he can hold her hand, and Ruth tells him if'n he wants ta hold her hand, he can take it like it is. She never has ta bear his advances 'cause he ain't agoin' ta make any as long as he feels she's dirty.

"Anyway, here he comes today with his two black henchmen. He wants ta talk ta Ruth. 'Course she's out in the bunkhouse by now. He starts his talk all over again. He sees little Sarah and reaches out to touch her with one finger of his lily white glove. I ain't sure what he's afraid of but it's a pure blind with him. Anyway, along comes Ruth and he's still atellin' her ta wash herself and all of a sudden ya hear that mule bray and then this crash and another bray and horses screamin' and wagons rollin', and they all jump to their feet and go to the window. Mr. Lord starts yellin' about germs and dirt and then ya see the buggy go tearin' off down the road and Mr. Lord gets hysterical. Wal, them two black garbed fellers jest take off down the road after the buggy and I hear Luke and Mose runnin' after them too. I went out on the porch jest in time ta see the buggy do a flip in the ditch. Wal, I begun ta laugh and Ruth begun ta laugh, and Mr. Lord became so hysterical ya couldn't understand a word he was sayin'. By the time the boys got back with the buggy he was almost voiceless. I couldn't stop laughin', and jest watchin' them fellers tryin' ta dust off that buggy for that over-clean dude…jest tickled me almost ta death. That poor man, still don't know what really happened ta him or who was ta blame. I'm still laughin' and I think it will give me pleasure for a long time to come."

Jake couldn't help laughing too, even though he felt he lost his opportunity to learn more about the man through Ruth's help.

They laughed and talked about it all during supper preparations. Ruth disappeared to return with the baby. She was a beautiful child and Jake tried to get her to warm up to him. She was just learning to walk and he and Ruth had great fun getting her to run back and forth between the two of them.

After supper, Jake and Ruth took a long walk. Ruth once again tried to make Jake see that she loved him.

"Ruth, honey, I cannot accept your love, nor can I allow you to attach your life to mine. As I told you before, it would only mean heartache for you."

"Jake, I want to ask you a question. This Mr. Lord seems to think you have placed a large sum of money in my name. I went to the bank and they said not. But Mr. Lord had been so persistent with his questioning about you that it bothers me. I know you have brought in several loads of gold ore and I do not know or care what you have done with it, but I do wish you'd take care, for I feel a chill wind when I lay alone at night and someone whispers your name in my dreams."

Jake stopped and stared at her. "Don't let your imagination get away from you, girl. Nothing's going to happen to me now, nothing." They turned toward the ranch house. At the door Jake bade her good night. She leaned forward and kissed him.

He returned to the bunkhouse and threw himself down on his bed. His thoughts were varied this night, tumbling and rolling through his head. Somehow he had to locate someone to help him find out more about this mysterious Mr. Lord. He had to do that man in for he was sure he was the one to blame for Pete's death and his robbery. Many hours later Jake was deep in thought and the moon had climbed high in the sky, casting its milky white glow across the bunkhouse floor.

The door opened and Ruth floated into the room. She stood bathed in moonlight, looking like an angel dressed in her white robe and gown.

Jake shot bolt upright.

"Ruth, my God, what are you doing here?"

She went over and sat down beside him on his bed.

"Jake, I know I'm a shameless hussy for what I'm about to do but I want to share my love with you. You will not accept my love forever and I will never love like this again. I know you have never experienced love before, and I want to be the one who lets you touch its beauty."

She lifted the covers and slid in beside him.

"Ruth, no! Oh, Ruth, you must not do this," he said as he enclosed her in his arms.

CHAPTER TWENTY-NINE

THE SUN WAS high when Jake awoke. He was also alone. Had he dreamed Ruth had been there, or had she really lay beside him in the moonlight? Yes, she had really been there. There were a couple of long blond hairs on his pillow. Lying back he remembered her lips, her hands caressing his back as he entered her. He trembled as the feeling warmed his soul. He also suddenly remembered Mr. Lord. Damn, he better get up and get busy. There was much to find out before heading home and he better hurry. First he had to contact Paul.

Paul greeted him excitedly. "Hey, Jake, oh boy, Jake, I sure am glad ta see ya. Thought ya never were comin'. Got a lot ta tell ya. Don't know how important it is, but it's somethin'."

Jake dismounted and placing an arm around the boy, said, "It's good to see you again, Paul. Where can we go where we won't be disturbed?"

"Out in the hay shed, I'm about the only one that goes out there so we can probably be alone there. How have ya been, Jake? Did ya find any more gold? Been wonderin' what ya were doin'. You're my only friend. Kinda been worrin' too. Heard some things that kinda scared me."

"I've been fine, Paul, and yes, I found more gold. Speaking of gold, I brought you a present." He took a large piece of ore out of his pocket and gave it to Paul. It had a small but clear vein of gold running through it.

"Oh, Gawd damn, Jake, will ya look at that. I'm gonna keep it forever."

They reached the shed and climbed to a fairly high spot where they could see if anyone was coming their way. Settling themselves into the hay, they began to catch up on all of the gossip of Carson City.

"Well, first off, Jake, when they meet there in the livery stable, I have to be so far up in the loft, it's hard to hear what they say. I found out one thing though. They are the ones that give Cecil the money and send him off to town to get drunk so they can meet in the livery stable while no one's around. Cecil was always afraid that if they came in and found no one guarding the team, they would fire him. But they know his weakness for liquor and they knew if they gave him enough money, he would go out and get himself drunk. So they never knew I was there. Cecil always gave me a quarter to stay all night and guard the team.

"What he didn't know was that I could never show myself to Mr. Lord. He hates me because I'm crippled. And besides, I would be able to hear what was being said. Now, right after you left, there was some man who came from Bodie. Don't know his name but he belonged to some gang run by a fellow named Vic. It was all about runnin' Chinese slaves. Somehow someone had turned them loose. Mr. Lord went crazy. Then's when I heard your name mentioned. Seems like he's out to really get you good. He says yer always meddlin' in the middle of his business, causin' him to lose all kind of deals. He says, 'We gotta get that humpback bastard out of the way.' I guess ya

188

must of really done somethin' to him."

"Well, Paul, I guess what I'm not personally responsible for, I've been at least mixed up in the end results. What else did you hear?"

"I don't know people around here very good, at least the women folk. Mr. Lord is always talkin' about the land deal you loused up. Somethin' about him courtin' some gal that belongs ta you. You don't have a gal, do ya, Jake?"

"Not in the sense of the word you're talking about. But I do know who he means. Do you know the Garrett ranch out on the outskirts of town?"

"Sort of. I knew Mr. Garrett some. He used to come into the stable with his team and buggy when he came to town. He was always pleasant to me, even though he was so sick. Mr. Lord put on quite a parade fer him. They packed his body right down main street. I hearsay that his funeral was special, but then, it wasn't him that was special, it was his ranch Mr. Lord's got his eye on."

"Have you heard, by any chance, why that piece of property is so important to him?"

"I think what he's lookin' fer is a sort of headquarters. He keeps talkin' about some place to meet that could get them in out of the dirt, one that was close enough in that could be gotten in and away from fast. Yet far enough away that it wouldn't be suspicious."

"I don't know, Paul, I still have a feeling that there is more to it than meets the eye. A man like that would have to have more of a reason than just a hideout but for the life of me, I can't figure what it would be. What else have you heard?"

"Wal, I hear he got himself in a real sweat yesterday. Even got himself dirty. He came back from courtin' that gal and he was just a railin'. The whole buggy was covered with dirt and the grays were sweat and dirt caked. Cecil said he was stormin' and callin' those two clods he has with him all kinds of names.

Poor Cecil has been workin' the team and buggy over for a day and a half. He makes me sick, Mr. Lord does. He won't set foot in the stables to touch one of his beautiful horses. Won't climb into the buggy even though Cecil has it spotless, unless one of his goons wipes it with a hanky."

"Guess you can blame me for that episode too, Paul, or at least old Blaze. He sure raised hell with those grays. Anything else you can tell me?"

"No, I cain't say I heard much more. I do know yer name comes up quite often and that worries me. I was afraid ya would end up shot before ya got back to Carson City."

"As a matter of fact, I did, but they didn't stay around to see if they finished the job. Well, son, I'd better be getting back to the ranch, get my gear together and go home to Bodie."

"Bodie? So that's where ya live, and that's where ya got all that gold yer always packin' in. I hear gold is stickin' right up outta the ground and ya can just reach down and pick it up. Is that true?"

"Hardly. Pickin' gold is heart-breakin', back-breakin', soul-rackin' work. Some of them miners out there have been workin' their life away and not made a dime worth keepin'. What they do find, they spend gamblin' or drinkin'. It's a rough life out in the gold fields. Rough!"

They climbed down out of the hay shed and Jake mounted Blaze and turned toward the ranch.

As he rode through town he thought of Bodie and his mine. *Maybe I'd better stop and buy a couple cases of dynamite. I need to open up that mine some.* He swung on over to the general store. While there, he met some of the miners that had been on the wagon train through the desert. They had a happy reunion, talking about the years that had passed since they had seen each other.

It was much later that Jake left for the ranch. When he arrived, he found his wagon and mules all hitched up, all but

Blaze whom he was riding. What the hell was going on? Then he saw a small pony and Paul. Ruth came running to meet him as he pulled into the yard. "Jake, oh, Jake, you must leave right now. Mr. Lord has found out that you're still alive and to blame for yesterday's misadventure."

"What's Paul doing out here, and what's that blood all over his head?"

"He beat me up, Jake, one of his men saw us comin' out of the hay shed. He came and got me and took me to the funeral parlor. They asked me all kinds of questions about you and when I told them to go to hell, they beat up on me. Then Mr. Lord screams, 'Go kill that son-of-a-bitch before he leaves the ranch.' I ducked out, grabbed the pony and headed for here. Seems funny that they haven't showed up yet."

Jake dismounted and began stripping the saddle from Blaze. He had a creepy feeling running up his back. Ruth kept chattering away about the two henchmen, Mr. Lord's fury, but Jake was only about half listening.

He hitched Blaze to the wagon and turned to Ruth. "Ruth, honey, you're right, I gotta be leavin' right now, I hope I'm not too late already."

He swung up into the wagon and turned the mules around, stopping at the gate to lean down to Ruth.

"Listen to me, Ruth, I have left you a great deal of money in the bank. Upon my death, it is yours and little Sarah May's. Please be careful and take care of yourself for I feel I shall not see you again. You must make a new life for yourself and the baby. I'm not part of it. What money I make from my mine, I shall take with me out of Bodie. Take care of Mrs. Garrett and remember me kindly, do you hear?"

Tears streaming down her face, she nodded her head. Jake's heart was tearing in two but he had to do this for Ruth's own sake.

Paul looked adoringly at Jake, his eyes filled with tears.

"Take me with ya, Jake. Please take me with ya. I ain't got nobody and I'm afraid to go back."

Jake leaned over and stretched out his hand to Paul. "Come on, boy, jump aboard and let's get outta here."

Jake turned the mules toward the miller ranch, he had an idea. There was an old wagon road leading out through the backcountry that Mr. Miller used to haul his hay to other ranchers. It was much used by many wagons and the tracks of his would be lost in the maze. All he needed was a place to hide until they could safely travel by night. Some yards later, the road as such ended and wagon tracks took off in all directions. They headed down one that went through a gate and ahead Jake could see a hay shed where hay was stored until it could be shipped. He drew the wagon to a stop and pulled it around front where it could not be seen by approaching traffic. Jake backed the wagon up into the hay to try to wedge it into the haystack, but it was packed heavy and hard. They got down from the wagon and unhitched the mules which could be hidden simply by turning them loose. They, themselves could burrow into the hay. The mules wandered off to roll and Jake and Paul dug in.

The hours dragged by. They never did hear approaching horses or signs of anyone. Just at dusk, Jake crawled out to look for the mules. They were only a short distance away. Once hitched, Jake headed out in the direction of the desert. He was having trouble for there were no trails from here to where he wanted to go, and it was beginning to get dark. Pulling over to a small outcropping of rocks, he stopped and Jake produced some of the food Ruth had packed for him, and he and Paul ate.

It was going to be a bright night with an early full moon. Jake and Paul climbed back into the wagon and headed rapidly for Bodie, wagon bumping along furiously over the rocky terrain. After a few short hours, the land smoothed out and they made better time. The moon was high by the time they reached the main road to Bodie.

CHAPTER THIRTY

THE TRIP HOME was uneventful and they saw nothing of Mr. Lord's henchmen. This worried Jake somewhat for he was sure this meant some other form of evil from the men. Three and a half days later, they pulled into Bodie where Jake bought meager supplies and picked up his mail. There was a large envelope from Texas and Jake could hardly wait to get home to read it.

It was late afternoon and Bodie was beginning to liven up for the evening. Paul was spellbound as he watched all the excitement. Jake could see lights at the placer mine on the hill and wondered how come it was going day and night.

As they headed off around the hill, he saw where there had been a fire and the old dance hall and Nugget Saloon were burned to the ground. He wondered where Lola was and if she had escaped. Things were sure happening here.

Jake pulled the wagon into Pete's old camp. There they unhitched, put the supplies across the mules and walked up to Jake's hut. On the long miles home Paul had said little or nothing. He was wide-eyed and bewildered by it all. He looked around Jake's hut in despair. It looked bleak, even to his young eyes. Jake watched him.

"That's all right, boy, once you spend a Sierra winter in this snug little hut, you'll change your mind. 'Course, it'll get kinda wet sometimes too, but we got a nice long summer ahead of us and hot is what you'll feel most." They set the supplies away and Jake sent Paul out to care for the mules while he dropped to his bunk to read his letter:

> *Dear Jake,*
>
> *Well, I promised you I'd write and tell you what I found. Hope this finds you still alive and in good health. I found the wagon about a day out. Mrs. Dunning and Jessie were driving. There were just three of them left, Jake. The youngest boy was leading the sheep and the wagon with all the good gold which was still intact. We are all at the old Dunning ranch now. Jessie and me are married now and running a nice little spread of cattle. You'd better get outta there, Jake, while you still can. Come join us. There's always room for you here. Thanks for everything.*
>
> *I remain your friend,*
> *Robert Faulkner*

Jake lay back in his bunk. He was glad to hear that news. At least all of Pete's hard labor in Bodie was not lost, and his widow would live an easier life now. It was a dirty shame, though, that he and all of his family could not enjoy the easier life. Jake felt the pain of emptiness in his heart left by Pete's passing. He figured that perhaps he had better make this his last year in this damnable hellhole. He could take his diggings and half of what was in the bank and relax for the rest of his life.

Then there was Paul, another reason to leave. He really was not too happy at the prospect of having the boy with him. This town was no place for a youngster. And what was he going to do with him when he pulled out of here? He was a nice enough boy and seemed to worship him. There was a deep feeling between them from the start and Jake could relate to his unhappiness due to his deformity. He had been through that himself. The boy was more fortunate than he was, though, for he had only a clubfoot. The rest of his young body was healthy. He had great masses of curly light brown hair that always needed to be brushed, although a currycomb would be more beneficial. He needed to be introduced to the everyday routine of personal hygiene. Jake figured a bar of soap and a toothbrush was a good start. Jake had to admit he was feeling the edges of love for the boy. It felt good to be needed and to need someone. He began to plan ahead for Paul's future. With the gold he had and could mine the rest of the year, he could really set the boy up for the rest of his life. See to it that he had good schooling so that he could be whatever he wanted to be. Actually, if he wanted to, he could leave now and still be a wealthy man but digging for gold was a fever in Jake's blood that was almost impossible to cool down. Were it not so, he would have been gone from Bodie long ago.

Jake had long dreamed of returning to Philadelphia a wealthy man, to show his family, his many foster families and all of the people who made his life miserable all those heartbreaking years of his youth. To get even and show those people who had been the driving force most of his life. Now it all seemed far away and useless.

Paul came in from caring for the mules. He walked shyly over and sat on the corner of the fireplace facing Jake. The candle glow cast a soft light on the two. Jake sat up and spoke. "How about some supper, my friend?"

"Fine with me, Jake."

"Okay, you bring in some wood and start a fire and I'll rustle up some food."

After the supper was cleared away, Jake pulled Paul up beside him and began asking questions, trying to find out more about the boy.

Paul was born in Carson City, the only child of Clara and Al Lamply. Al was the town drunkard at the time and was extremely cruel while under the influence of drink. His wife was a meek, sniveling woman and bore the brunt of his drunken ravings. They said he beat her so much that she didn't have any mind left, and the night Paul was born, he had beaten her unmercifully.

When little Paul was born with his deformed foot, the blame was placed on his father. Paul's mother had died at his birth and his father had placed him with the midwife who delivered him and silently disappeared forever.

Paul's grandfather worked on a ranch some twenty miles out of town and when he heard about the boy, he came and took Paul home with him. His grandfather was a stern man and bordered on cruelty himself and Paul had never known a day of happiness or ease. He had never been to school and knew nothing but work in all the twelve years of his life.

Maybe he could give the boy the love he longed to give and make the rest of his days as happy as it was possible for him to do. He reached over and put his arm around the boy and drew him close. As he did so, Paul broke into sobs, cleansing his soul of his past.

CHAPTER THIRTY-ONE

THE FOLLOWING DAYS were spent opening the mine and preparing for work. Jake was sure there was a sizeable vein of ore running deeper into the hill and he figured when he and Paul finished working what was open, he would dynamite and see if he could open it up.

Paul was a hard worker despite his age and foot. Together they drew load after load of dirt and rock out of the mine. The vein was growing smaller and smaller and the pile of dirt and rock grew larger and larger. Jake took a look at it one day and knew he was making it known to all that passed by that gold was there. He missed Cad. That was one thing he was good at, getting rid of the overflow. It made him nervous and he made frequent trips outside to scan the countryside.

It was once again time to stock up on supplies. They did not last long with a growing boy to feed. They pulled the camouflage screen across the mine entrance and left for Bodie. They passed many people on the road, Bodie was booming and people were coming and going with regularity. There had been another fire while Jake and Paul had been working. One of the churches had burned almost before it was finished being built. The town teemed with miners and gambling halls ran full blast all day and night.

It was all bright and exciting for Paul who gazed around him with open mouth and sparkling eyes. They walked all through town with Jake showing Paul what there was to see. They lingered in gambling halls so Paul could see the wheels at work. All were crowded, noisy and smoke filled. At one place, there was a stage where entertainment ran twenty-four hours a day. The girls were flamboyant, underdressed, over painted and looked tired out, but to Paul, they were a beautiful sight.

They ate at the café, bought supplies, but before heading for home, Paul talked Jake into visiting the dance hall again. While they were there, Jake spied a familiar figure, Lola. He told Paul to stay put and started to work his way through the crowd to her. As he pushed a large miner out of his way, he saw two men approach her and they headed for the far corner. He stopped and stared. They looked familiar to him, very familiar. They were Mr. Lord's henchmen! That meant only one thing, trouble! Lola looked frightened and uneasy.

Jake turned and worked his way back to Paul. Nudging him he said, "Look yonder, boy, do you see what I see?"

Paul started, "Let's get the hell outta here. They'll kill us on sight."

They moved out and headed for the wagon. The way home was silent and fear had taken a toll on the pleasure of the day. As they approached Pete's old diggings where they stored the wagon, a shot rang out and a bullet shot against the metal framing of the wagon. The mules bolted and both Jake and Paul sprang from the wagon to head for cover. They crouched behind the rocks and tried to locate which direction the shot came from. Jake could not see anyone across the road, behind or up on the hill.

There were no more shots and cautiously Jake went for the team. He scanned the hillside as he did but still could not locate the area from which the shot came. He unhitched the mules and placed the packs upon their backs and loaded them with supplies. They then headed the mules up to the hut. As they turned on the path to head up the hill, another shot rang out and ricocheted off a boulder. This time Jake could almost spot the area. *Hell,* he thought, *they're damn near in back of the hut.*

What the hell was going on? Just then a man emerged from the hut, firing as he ran. One of the bullets hit Moonshine and he dropped to the ground with a moan. "Gawd damn!" shouted Jake, jumping to his feet and blasting out with his rifle. Too late, they were already out of sight.

"Them sons-a-bitches!" cried Paul, "them dirty sons-a-bitches!"

"Easy there, Paul, that's awful strong language for a boy your age."

"I don't give a damn, they shot Moonshine. Jesus, what they wanna go and do a thing like that fer?" Paul reached down and put his arms lovingly around the mule's neck. And at that moment, Moonshine lifted his head and heaved himself to his feet. The bullet had gashed a deep gash in his shoulder. Otherwise, he seemed unscathed. Paul sat there on the ground and stared at him. "These are two smart mules, what other animals do you know that would be smart enough to hit the ground that way? He looks all right other than that gash. We can fix that up with a little of Pete's famous sheep fat. Let's go see what they found in the hut."

The little hut was a mess. Things were scattered everywhere and turned upside down, all but the screen over the entrance to the mine. Jake blew air out of his mouth. "Phew! That's a relief. I'm afraid there's no stopping that bunch now that they know where I live." They would keep at him until they found the mine. That pile of dirt and rock was a pure dead giveaway.

They'd have to be stupid not to figure that one out. This time he had come home a little earlier than expected, that's all. Staying at home was not an option anymore. They could take him out at any time.

Perhaps now was the time to pack up and get out. Yeah, well, maybe so, but that vein was still sizeable enough to keep his fever burning. It had to open up further on, he was positive. It had to. He ran his fingers through his hair and paced the floor. He gave himself the excuse that he had more obligations than Ruth now, with Paul. He would not listen to his common sense telling him that he had ample money right now to fulfill his self-imposed obligations.

He went outside to help Paul put the mules away and to administer to Moonshine's wound. They were a beautifully matched team that worked well together and he certainly did not want to lose them.

CHAPTER THIRTY-TWO

AFTER SUPPER, JAKE walked outside in the twilight. His eyes swept the landscape for campfires. There were many that belonged to the recent influx of miners but none in any suspicious places. He walked to the top of his hill and gazed east. He could see many spirals of smoke. It would be hard to place any of them as a special camp of outlaws.

He pondered his position. If they were deep in the mine working, they would never hear footsteps of someone approaching. Also, the mouth of the mine would be open and the element of surprise would be total. Somehow they were going to have to work this out. He turned and looked at the work pile. Maybe they should do a little outside digging to make it look as if they were trying to mine the hillside.

He went after Paul. In the soft evening light and early night, the two dug a sizeable hole, scattering dirt and rock in the direction of the existing pile. The following morning early they were at it again. Paul actually did find some color and he worked the rest of the day in that one spot. The spot never did become large enough to become a vein, but kept crisscrossing itself while making a slow course toward the shack. Jake suspected it was a branch off of the original mine inside.

They had quite a pile of rocks by noon and they lay down the picks and worked out of the rock Paul had dug. It was more scales than nuggets and made a pitifully small bag by nightfall. To Paul it was a grand haul and gold fever struck hard within his breast. This was his strike and he was wild with excitement. If Jake had let him, he would have dug by lantern light the rest of the night.

"Say, Jake," spoke Paul as he ate, "what say, do ya suppose I should sleep out there on my mine with a rifle? Someone might come along and steal it, mighten they? It ain't very big now but it'll get richer as I go along. I think I outta protect it."

"Now, Paul, nobody's gonna steal your mine tonight. Nobody even knows it's there yet. So you just sleep in your bunk for tonight and let's see what tomorrow brings."

Now, if that yellow washed rock keeps going out there, I ain't ever going to get Paul back into the big one, Jake chuckled to himself. All kidding aside, Jake was extremely uneasy. The two men that were caught at the hut were obviously not the two henchmen of Mr. Lord's. Did that mean they were looking for loose gold, or were they new men hired by Mr. Lord? They had found nothing the first time and no one showed up all day but Jake felt it was not over. In fact, he felt it had really just begun.

Paul went out to check on his strike three more times before settling in for the night. Jake slept with the shotgun in his hand. He was conscious of every little noise and each one sounded like someone stealing up to the door. It made a long night.

Next day, Paul was up before the sun and Jake could hear the ring of his pick. He made a fire, put the coffee on, took his rifle and wandered outside. It was going to be a blasting hot day. The air was already hot and the sun was not up yet.

Looking around he could see activity even this early. There were people on the road and he could see spirals of smoke from campfires all over the hills. It would be impossible to locate intruders.

He looked at Paul. "Say boy, you ain't gonna be able to work too long out here soon as the sun's up."

"That's why I gotta work hard now," said Paul, swinging his pick high above his head.

By the time Jake got the mules fed and breakfast ready the sun was up. Jake hesitated, listening. Paul had stopped picking. *When had he stopped?*

Fear gripped him. Picking up his rifle, he walked outside. There was Paul looking at each piece of rock he had dug.

"What's the matter, Paul?"

Paul looked up with tears in his eyes. "Gone, Gawd damn it, gone. I been picking all mornin' and now that the sun's up, thar ain't no more color. I been pickin' fer nothing."

Jake could almost have laughed except for the look of defeat on Paul's face. How many times in how many states had this happened to him? He put his arm around Paul's shoulder saying, "Come on in and have your breakfast, son. We have so many things we need to be doing so we can get ourselves out of this place. It's getting unhealthier by the day. I can't see anyone but I feel they are out there. The hair stands up on my head all of the time."

That day they spent inside in the mine. The vein was getting weaker and beginning to split. He wondered if he should place a stick or two of dynamite to open up a richer vein. First they had better clean up the two smaller ones.

Later that day he walked out to where he had the smelting pot covered. He looked at the countryside. If he were to stoke up the fires for the pot, he could possibly be seen. *I guess maybe the best thing for me to do would be to hitch old Blaze to the drag cart and drag the damn thing back down to Pete's old smelting shed and give up smelting anymore of my ore. It would be easier and faster to just haul bags of dust and ore in the wagon.*

He hitched up the mule, fastened him to the drag and he and Paul went bumping and pinging down the hill to the road. On the way up to Pete's place, Jake saw a movement in the dry wash. Suddenly someone stood but just before Jake could get off a shot, Lola screamed, "Jake, wait! Don't shoot me, please!"

"What in God's name are you doing down here, woman?"

"Oh, Jake, help me, please help me," she pleaded. She stooped over and picked up an old ragged red flowered carpetbag. It was then he noticed she was dressed in dark traveling clothes with good sturdy boots on her feet.

"Where do you think you're going, Lola? You can't walk anywhere in weather like this. You'll have heat stroke."

"I've gotta get outta here, Jake. I've jest gotta! They're gonna kill me and I cain't let that happen. Please, please help me."

"Why should I help you? You've been the key to so many deaths and robberies. I couldn't count them all. The only thing anyone would help you with is an early demise."

Lola's face began to take on a hard look, then softened. She needed this man and it behooved her to play it safe.

"Aw, come on, Jake, be a sport. I really need help."

Jake squinted his eyes and stared at her. "Wellll...I'll do what I can. Where are you going and how did you think you were going to get there? It's dead of summer and the desert is no place for a man this time of year, let alone a woman."

"I don't know, I really didn't plan too much. I know that somewhere around Mono, the stage does through and I can go to Sacramento and then catch the train for San Francisco. I hear it's quite a town to get lost in and I'm sure there's a place fer a girl like me."

"I'll bet there is. A woman like you can smell a con game anywhere."

Jake sighed, "Well. That's a hell of a long way to walk. And if they're looking for you, you'd stick out like a fly in a milk bucket. Let's go over and drop the pot and we'll talk about it some more. We're too much in the open here."

They dragged the pot on over to Pete's place and stuck it back up in the rocks. Pete's old lean-to offered them shade to sit and talk. Jake placed his rifle across his lap and scanned the hillside for movement. He never took his eyes off the hills or the road as they talked.

Listening to Lola's life story made him sick. She was rotten through and through. She started out as a child thief, worked into learning the con game with a couple of gamblers. She then went on to prostitution, selling female flesh, and teaming up with Mr. Lord. Maybe he would be doing the world a favor if he just let her stay and take her medicine. But he couldn't do that and live with himself either. It was Mr. Lord he wanted and maybe this would flush him out.

Jake sat quietly for a long time. He thought of Pete and his family, and who knew how many other miners and their families, lost their fortune and their lives because of this woman. Bodie would probably be glad to see one of their problems disappear.

Perhaps he could hitch up the wagon, but then there was Moonshine who could no more work in harness with that gash across his shoulder than he could. There were the two smaller mules, they would pull all right but they would be much slower. Plus, he could not depend on quick response when he needed it. He could keep Lola at the hut until Moonshine's wound healed but then she would know the position of his mine. If she were caught after she boarded the stage, he was sure she would divulge the secret rather than die. Still, she could not do him any harm if she were miles away in San Francisco. But then, if

205

they had dreamed this all up and this was a trap to catch him…if, if, if, if. What the hell was he going to do?

Lola sat looking at him as if she knew the conflict going on inside him.

Jake sighed, "Well, I don't know what to say, Lola. I've got problems where helping you are concerned. I could hitch up my wagon and drive you over to the state line, but my one mule is laid up and the two smaller ones are lazy and slow. They work very well if old Blaze and Moonshine are leading. They haven't much choice with those two. I could also take you home to the hut until Moonshine healed, but that would be another kind of a problem. Besides, if they should find you there, it would be a bad thing for all of us." He got up and called for Paul to hike up the hill in back of the hut where he could see and watch it.

Paul took off scrambling over the rocks as best he could. Before he reached the top, they saw him duck behind a large boulder. They waited, Paul came back down, hunching behind rocks as he came. Crossing the road and out of breath, he panted, "Somebody's at the hut, Jake. Cain't see the feller, but thar's a mule standin' thar."

Jake got up and checked his rifle. "Paul, you stay here with Lola and I'll go see what's going on."

Jake followed the dry wash down to the foot of the path up to the hut. He then cautiously began to climb up through the rocks. He saw the mule and stood up in relief. It belonged to the miner who lived over the hill from him. He went into the hut to find Saul Winters all dressed up fine.

"What are you doing over here, Saul?"

The man turned, he had a chunk of ore from Jake's mine in one hand. "Looks like yer vein's playin' out, Jake. Gol durn, who'd ever suspect yer minin' yer own gol dang house. Been over ta town, Jake, getting ready ta blow the dust of these hills from ma' boots. Heard some talk. Yer name was sorta brought up by these fellers and it didn't sound ta me like they were singin' a love song about ya. I also stopped ta pick up my mail and thought I'd pick yers up and meander over. Don't know if ya need warnin' or not on them fellers, but here's yer mail anyhow." He handed Jake a small white envelope and Jake knew it was Ruth before opening it up.

My Dearest Jake:
Today we buried Aunt Sarah. My heart lies heavy in my breast. I am once again alone, except for little Sarah. I do not know if this letter will reach you in time or not. Mr. Lord has been pushing for my hand in marriage again. He's furious because I told him of my love for you and my hatred of him. He is on his way over to kill you, Jake. Oh, how I pray this letter reaches you before he does. Please watch yourself and take care. I wish you would leave that awful place and come to me here. The house and property are mine now and we could live here happily, I'm sure. I had a dream again the other night and I fear for you, Jake. Please consider my offer for I love you. Ruth.

Jake's heart pounded, the thought of being with Ruth the rest of his life thrilled him, but he could not. He had made other plans now and they did not include Ruth.

"Saul, when are you leavin' these parts?"

"Right away, Jake. Why?"

"I was wonderin', I've got to take a lady over to the stage line the other side of Mono Lake and I sure would be beholden' to you if you would stay here at the hut until I get back?"

"That ain't no problem, man, I'll jest pick up my belongings and come right on over."

Jake hurried down the hill to where he left Paul and Lola. He told them about Saul and that he was going to watch the hut

207

until they got back. "And perhaps Saul will lend me his mule to hitch up front with Blaze so I can have a faster more dependable team. We could then leave outta here by dusk tonight and be down there before the stage. Then Paul and I can be back here by dusk tomorrow night. Lola, you stay here under the lean-to far enough back so you can't be seen from the road and we'll be back to pick you up."

He and Paul went back to the hut. Saul was still gone and Jake set about making preparations for the trip. He checked Moonshine again, dressed his wounds and made a small supper. He sent Paul down with some food for Lola. After Paul had gone, he sat down and read Ruth's letter again and suddenly felt another chill of fear. He looked around him. All was quiet. He walked outside, looking around the area, still no one. But the chill was still there and was to remain with him for some time.

Toward late afternoon Saul returned with two packed mules and riding a third. As Saul dismounted, Jake asked, "Say, Saul, would you mind if I borrowed your riding mule? I need a four-mule team and Moonshine is laid up with a bullet wound."

"Sure, Jake, I don't mind a bit. Say, what air ya all up to anyway?"

Jake hastily explained the mission, then was duly sorry.

"Gawd damn, man, I wouldn't help that murderin' schemin' bitch with nothin'. The only good thing I kin say is yer gettin' her outta the territory and *that* alone will probably save a lot of lives. 'Course, ya kin do that by simply slittin' her throat." Saul was stomping around the room waving his arms while talking.

Jake grinned, looks like Lola's fame was wide spread. She was probably leaving before some other miner could do just that. Saul kept raving. "Gawd damn, Jake, I thought ya was helpin' a lady. She ain't no lady. If'n I'd know'd it was Lola, I doubt I'd have promised ta watch yer hut. Jesus, she ain't nothin' but a slut of the worst kind. How could ya do it? I got a good mind ta pull out now and let ya sweat it out."

Jake pulled Saul back and sat him down. "Now, Saul, you sit right here and listen to me. I ain't thinking so much about her as I am the rest of us."

"Wal, still don't like it, still think she's a slut but I guess all she-cats are the same when they turn hard and bad."

The two men rounded up Jake's other mules and fed them all a nosebag full of grain. Jake then led them down to Pete's where Paul helped him hitch them to the wagon. Jake couldn't help feeling much the same as Saul about Lola. Jake kept watching the hills and the road. The chill he felt earlier was even stronger and it was turning into a foreboding. As the time drew nearer for them to leave, the chill turned into a knot of fear in the pit of his stomach. He finally could stand it no longer. "Come on, let's get the hell out of here now."

Paul looked at him and instantly picked up the fear that filled Jake. "Yer expectin' trouble, ain't ya, Jake?"

"I guess you might say that, boy. I brought an extra rifle. Think you can handle it for me? We might need it before the night's through."

He packed Lola's belongings under the seat of the wagon and they climbed in with Paul facing the road behind. Jake turned the mules around and they headed for Mono Lake. He kept the mules at a trot and his eyes on the horizon. Jake spoke to Paul over his shoulder. "Keep your eyes peeled back there, boy, and tell me if you see anything coming up from behind. And keep your rifle handy."

Paul sat straight up and puffed himself up with a feeling of importance. Dusk overtook them before they reached the bottom of the hill and it was dark by the time they reached the Mono turnoff. The feeling of fear never left Jake and now, with it being pitch dark, the hair was standing up at the nape of his neck. Never before had he been so aware of the yapping of coyotes. They seemed so close he kept the mules trotting along at a fast clip. The road from Mono Lake to the stage stop at Mono was a wide, well-traveled road and easy to follow, even in the dark of night.

Dawn was beginning to break by the time they reached the stage stop at Mono and as they approached the outskirts of town, rifle shots rang through the clear morning air. Lola slumped forward and bullets whistled over their heads. Jake could see the fire from the rifles coming from a small shack and aimed his rifle for it. Both he and Paul fired into it repeatedly. The mules bolted and took off down the road at a gallop. By the time Jake could get them stopped, they were through town and well on the other side.

As he pulled them to a stop, he spied a rig across the way in a small ravine with two dapple gray horses hitched to it. A wave of bitter hot fury ran through his veins and grabbing the rifle Paul had just finished loading, paying no attention to anything else, started firing at random. Again the mules bolted, throwing Jake backwards and by the time he got righted, the buggy was gone.

"Damn! Damn! Damn!" shouted Jake, throwing his rifle to the ground and grabbing the reins to stop the mules. He stood up, pulling the team around to start up the ravine.

He saw Paul standing in the road where he had evidently fallen off when the mules bolted. "Wait, Jake, wait. Ya ain't gonna catch that buggy goin' up that ravine. It's too narrow. Look."

Jake stopped, sitting down hard on the seat and putting his head in his hands. He looked down on the floor to see Lola lying there. He had forgotten her in his rage. Paul ran up to the wagon and looked at her. "She's daid, ain't she, Jake?"

Jake rolled her over and put his fingers to her throat. "Yes, Paul, she's dead." He was still under the influence of rage and taking his foot he pushed her out onto the road, grabbed Paul, hauling him into the wagon and took off at a gallop.

CHAPTER THIRTY-THREE

SAUL'S SNORING CAME to an abrupt stop and he sat up with his rifle ready. "Who's thar?"

"It's us, Saul," Jake replied.

He and Paul unharnessed and fed the mules, bedding them down for the rest of the night. Paul was out on his feet and dropped onto his bunk already half asleep. Jake sat down on the end of his bunk and sighed.

Saul scurried around lighting a fire and putting the coffee pot on to boil. "What happened, Jake, man, ya look awful?"

Shaking his head, Jake replied, "God, it was awful, Saul. Lola is dead, several men are dead, and I almost had that bastard, 'Lord.' I almost lost the wagon and I am no better off than I was before. I now know for sure, it was a trap. Lola was the first one shot, so I know they were going to do her in for sure. Paul and I kept firing and firing and the mules bolted. While I was trying to get the wagon stopped, I saw the Lord buggy up a ravine. Things just got worse from there and I lost the opportunity to kill the son-of-a-bitch."

The remainder of the night was spent over cups of coffee while Jake related the whole story to Saul.

In the morning, Jake helped Saul pack his gear again and said, "Say, Saul, them two mules of Pete's are runnin' loose around here. They show up for grain every once in a while and are still right tame. Let's take a couple mules and see if we can locate them. That way you could ease the load on your two."

"Wal, I don't know, Jake, I got about all I kin handle with these three. I ain't strong in ma shoulders any more and it's quite a job fer me, hauling two behind me, and they ain't packed that heavy."

"What about your gold, Saul? Ain't you carryin' any out?"

"Hell no, man, do ya think I'm crazy? I never did get much but what I got did get through on some of those freight wagons to Sacramento and I aim ta get it outta the bank and head fer richer fields."

Jake looked hard at the old man. He guessed he'd be forever on the searching end of a gold strike. But then, so was he, except he was wasting his time on one spot.

The time went slowly by after Saul left. Jake was restless and he kept a steady stream of ore coming up out of his mine. One night he stood looking at the growing pile of quartz ore and decided he and Paul should pack it in bags and haul it down to the old abandoned cave he used before. That would take some of the worry off his back. Jake figured that the men who had located his mine before must have been killed the night of Lola's death for no one had bothered him since. Still, you never know when it will happen again.

Once that was accomplished, Jake left Paul to putter around in the mine while he went down to Pete's place to look at the wagon. It had gotten pretty banged around in Mono. He knew it needed a new wheel and some of the sideboards had to be replaced. He was becoming more and more disillusioned with Bodie, and Ruth's letter had set a spark of new hope in his breast. Also, the mine was getting poorer and poorer. There were a couple of veins away back in the shaft and maybe by dynamiting them, he could open up a richer pocket. Then he would have enough to think about moving on. Yeah! Right! He was the biggest jackass on the hill. He knew that if the vein were rich he never would leave. Or would he? If not, what was he doing fixing the wagon? Well, because he needed it to pack ore. On and on, his mind jumping from one avenue of escape to another avenue of high risk.

"What the hell am I going to do?" he cried.

Jake's tormented thoughts were interrupted by Paul as he came down the hill yelling, "Jake, Jake, guess what I found. I found all kinds of light veins headin' toward the back wall. Do ya suppose there's a great big one backa there?"

Jake lay down the 1 x 4 he was working on and took Paul's outstretched hand, allowing him to drag him back up the hill. He entered the mine and followed Paul's point to where it ended at the back wall.

"Damn, it sure looks like it could." Jake rubbed his beard. "Hmmm!" he mused. "I wonder if I could just blow enough of that wall away to hurry the process."

That night, he and Paul unpacked the box of dynamite he had purchased in Carson City. The mine ran down into the hill rather than going straight in and he figured that one stick of dynamite placed just right would do the trick without caving in the hill. He hurriedly fixed supper and by the time they finished, he was shaking and nervous. What was the matter with him?

Paul came up behind him and he jumped like a shot rabbit. "Say, Jake, what the hell's the matter with you anyhow? You're as jumpy as one of Mr. Lord's high-strung grays."

"I don't know, son," replied Jake as he placed a hand on the boy's shoulder. I've got chills and sweats and fears. I think we'd better blow that mine tonight while it's dark and get ourselves all we can out of this place and get outta this country."

They grabbed the box, lantern and fuses and headed down the steep shaft. Jake poked out a well-placed hole and inserted the stick of dynamite. He took an extra long fuse and just as he lit it a voice from in back of them said, "Well, I see that you are the ingenious one, Jake. Who but you would think of mining their own house?"

Jake swung around, knocking the box of dynamite out of Paul's hand, to see the infamous Mr. Lord, white gloves and all, standing in the mine entrance. He pushed Paul up the shaft and confronted Mr. Lord. "You better get the hell out of here if you want to live."

Grinning, Mr. Lord said, "Why don't you two get out of the way and let me see just what you have found that's so interesting."

Jake opened his mouth to warn him, then closed it again as a devious thought crossed his mind. "Sure, sure, I can see that I'm outwitted. Be my guest." He turned to Paul. "Get outta here now." Paul opened his mouth to say something and Jake pushed him hard out the entrance. Then grabbing his hand, dragged him out the front door and down the hill as fast as they could stumble.

There was a mighty blast and the hut blew into the air, mine, gold, Mr. Lord and all.

The force of the blast threw Jake and Paul to the ground, tumbling them over and over down the hill.

Jake stood and pulled Paul to his feet. "Are you all right, Paul? Here, turn around, let me check you out."

He dusted the boy off and checked out his limbs. Other than skinned elbows and knees, he was fine. He himself suffered a scrape along his humped spine but there did not seem to be anything broken.

Tears filled Paul's eyes. "Gone, Gawd damn, it's all gone.

Where's Blaze and the rest of the mules?"

"I brought them down here with me this afternoon when I came down to fix the wagon. Call that a lucky break. I don't know if there are anymore of Mr. Lord's men around but I think we had better hide ourselves over on the other side of Pete's smelting shed. There is a small dugout there where Pete used to hide his gold. Then tomorrow we'll finish fixing that wagon wheel and drop down to the cave, pick up our ore and come tomorrow night, we'll be on our way outta here."

They huddled in the dugout, Jake's arm around Paul, and he dreamed what he had never before allowed himself to dream. Ruth, her golden hair, her kisses and her moonlight visit. Dare he go to her? He closed his eyes and fell asleep.

The moon was full the following night and the wagon with only the gold ore and two people emerged onto the road to Carson City. Each had their dream of happiness as they followed the golden moon to their destiny.

THE END

Printed in the United States
1341900001B/243